THE WHITE CAMEL

THE WHITE CAMEL

Eden Phillpotts

Illustrated by

Sheikh Ahmed

Elliott & Thompson
London

CONTENTS

Introduction

I am so happy that this magical book is finally going to be made available once more. I discovered it through my literary agent, Serafina Clarke, who has been a tireless campaigner for the re-publication of the book for some years. I read it to my daughter who has now re-read it six times on her own and is a great fan.

It is a wonderful book for adults and children alike, written in a style which manages to be both intensely poetic and excitingly muscular at the same time. It is good to see a children's book written without a hint of condescension or any taint of political correctness (a flaw, I think, in many children's books today) and yet, from a cultural point of view, it rings perfectly true.

It is also a terrific adventure story in a kind of Arabian Nights tradition, and if my daughter is in any way typical of the young reading public, should have enormous success. I hope so. I too have become a fan and am delighted to see it back in print once again.

Joanne Harris

Chapter I

♦

Three Things Happen

Sheikh Abbas was a mighty man of valour who lived in Arabia and reigned over a clan of the Bedouin Arabs, leading them from place to place with their herds and flocks. His people feared him, but they always obeyed him because he was not a person you could say 'No' to very easily.

Now, when I speak of Arabia and tell you that the White Camel lived all his wonderful life there, you will say, 'Which Arabia?' Because there are three. Arabia the Stony is a land of mountains and fierce wadis, or river-valleys, where the great streams roar down in the rainy seasons and dry up again when the sun comes out to roast the world; Arabia the Blessed is the land of cities and farms and fruit and oil and honey and corn and sweet scents that make the air delicious to breathe; and Arabia the Sandy is a vast and burning desert, where strange things happen and strange folk dwell. Mountains thrust up out of the great ocean of sand, and scattered upon it sparingly are oases and wadis, where the precious water rises from far below and gives the trees and shrubs and grass a chance to live and prosper in the midst of that thirsty world.

Now Sheikh Abbas dwelt upon Arabia the Sandy; but he had a beautiful oasis of his very own in the midst of it. When he and his people were tired of wandering upon the great Red Desert of Dahna – to find the browse that their sheep and camels needed – he would break up his camp and take everybody back to his oasis, that the men and women and children and flocks might see the green of living things again, and drink sweet water from the wells, and eat fresh fruits and enjoy themselves, before they set out once more upon their restless wanderings. For the roaming Bedouins cannot stop in one place very long: they must be on the move and they would hate to be like the townsfolk and settle down in one house for evermore. They better love to dwell under their tents and wander amid the adventures and dangers of the eternal sand.

And now you meet the little clan of Sheikh Abbas, encamped two days' march from the oasis, under a low ridge of hills that ran between them and the eastern sky. It is the middle of the night, and the moon shines above the desert and makes the sandy wilderness all grey. Far out in the desert hyenas are laughing together and making a faint but horrid noise. What they are laughing about nobody can tell you, but they are rude fellows, with rather nasty manners, and I don't suppose their jokes would amuse us very much. The desert jackals are also breaking the great silence. They howl in rather a mournful fashion and don't sound as if they had much to laugh about; but they annoy the dogs of the camp, and the dogs bark back at them and tell them to shut up and run away.

Where is the camp itself? But for an accident you would hardly see it, for it is crouching under the low, dark hills, and there beneath their little tents, woven of goats' hair all dyed pitch black, dwell a large company of men and women; while round about the horses, camels and sheep are herded. At this time, in the dead of night, everybody would be asleep as a rule, except the watchmen standing with their spears and flint-lock guns to keep guard over the slumbering camp; but tonight, though the children are all sound asleep and the flocks and herds also, there is a rapid movement among the tents. Lights are flashing; men are hastening about and calling to each other; folk are alert and awake because much out of the common is happening.

Three things are in truth all happening together and they all three concern life and death. The most tremendous matter relates to Sheikh Abbas himself; because he is going to pass away. He is very old, and he is departing as he always lived, bravely and without fear. He has lived a stormy life and done a great deal of fighting in his time. He has been dreaded and very much disliked by a great many people, for he was never the sort of person that you can get to love;

Chapter I

but he has made his clan strong, governed them
sternly and harshly and taught them to be tough and
hard, like himself. He has lived rather a cunning life,
and told a good many lies in his time, but he lied and
deceived for the good of his people and their welfare,
and he has always tried to make them the strongest
folk in the desert. Sheikh Abbas was in fact a great
man, but not a very good one; and many people are
good though few are great, and very seldom do they
happen to be both. The Sheikh lay in the chieftain's
tent and his wise ones ministered to him and attend-
ed to his needs. He was really dying of old age, so
nothing could be done about it. His wives were all
dead long ago, for he had been very difficult to live
with and when the last passed away he said that he
was tired of having wives, and never married again.
No women were in his tent now; but his son, Heber,
sat beside him and held his hand, and the doctor of
the clan stood at his head and smoothed his pillow.
Then, feeling that his time was short, Sheikh Abbas
called for his sword, and they put a magnificent
weapon of Damascus steel into his hand. He passed
his fingers along the glittering blade, then lifted it
with both hands and passed it to his son, Heber.

'Wear it and use it,' he said.

Next he commanded that his horse should be
brought into the tent, that he might bid the beast
farewell, for he loved it much better than anything
else in the world. So they woke the Arab charger
from his sleep and told him that his master wanted
him, and he followed the messenger like a dog into
the chieftain's tent and stood beside him and lowered
his great head that Sheikh Abbas might pat him and

look into his eyes. He was a grand chestnut horse of fifteen hands high – a Nejdee horse, which is the very best sort that comes even from Arabia – and he had carried the Sheikh to victory in many a battle. He had been given to Sheikh Abbas by a sultan as a reward for helping him to conquer his enemies.

Now the old man pulled the horse's head to him and kissed it. Then he turned to Heber.

'Ride it and fight upon it,' he said.

The horse gave a little whinny and went back quietly to his place in the camp. His red coat gleamed ruby-bright under the lamps in the tent, but shone like silver when he stood out in the moonlight again. Presently he shut his beautiful eyes and slept – to dream perhaps of noble fights and desert tournaments and races, all of which he had enjoyed in his time.

The night waned slowly, and Sheikh Abbas asked for his dwarf. 'Bid Seyf come to me,' he said, and they fetched the dwarf, who sat beside his master and took Heber's place for a while. For Heber had another matter on his mind that night beside the passing of his father. The doctor also departed for a little while, to make some fresh medicine, and Sheikh Abbas turned to Seyf. The dwarf was well shaped and had a sharp, little, ratty face with a scrubby beard and beetle-black eyes; but he stood only three feet tall, though quite grown up. He was the only person in the clan who did not fear Sheikh Abbas, and never hesitated to answer him back and even argue with him. For this reason the Sheikh thought well of Seyf; and he was wont to say that the dwarf had more brains in his tiny little finger than all the rest of the clan put together.

CHAPTER I

Now the ancient man asked a question.

'Shall I go to heaven, dwarf?' he said.

And Seyf looked upon him tenderly and patted his old hand and answered,

'With Allah, dear master, all things are possible.'

This seemed to amuse Sheikh Abbas a little and he uttered a wish.

'I should enjoy a kangaroo-rat,' he told Seyf, 'so you had better call a dog or two and go and catch one.'

A kangaroo-rat is a funny little grey animal who lives in the desert, though what he manages to live upon nobody knows. He makes holes in the sand and pokes about and enjoys his life as much as we do. He hops like a kangaroo, because his hind legs are very long, and his real name is jerboa. The Arabs like to eat him for a change, and now Seyf called two dogs and went out into the moony desert to catch a jerboa.

The dogs were rather foxy fellows, much the colour of the sand, with sharp black noses and bright black eyes. You might have thought they were jackals, but they would have been very angry if you had told them so, because they hated jackals, just as so many people hate to think their great-great-great-grandfathers were not so fine as themselves, or to believe that their great-great-great-grandchildren will be finer. The dogs called themselves the friends of men and loved to be with men and do good work for the camp. They herded the flocks and kept away the bad beasts and often caught gazelles and hares for their masters, because they were splendid hunters and could run faster than any desert thing but one. There was one creature that could go quicker even than the Sheikh's Arab horse, though it only had two legs to his four, and that was the ostrich. For when an ostrich is really in a hurry, he runs like lightning and is very hard to catch.

Seyf and his dogs presently saw a little grey shadow hopping about in the moonlight, and a clever dog caught it, gave it one merciful shake and brought it to the dwarf. Then they all went back to camp, and soon a clever cook set to work to make a delicious stew of the jerboa for Sheikh Abbas. But when it was brought to him, he had grown too sick to eat it and soon afterwards he turned his face to the wall of the tent.

'Sleep and Death are brothers,' he said, 'and I fear the big brother no more than a little, weary child fears Sleep.'

Then came his son Heber with good news, for the second great thing in the camp had happened, just in time for Sheikh Abbas to hear about it before he departed.

'My wife has borne a man-child,' said Heber. 'He is a noble and perfect baby and all is well with him and his mother – my beloved Heart's Delight.'

'Give Allah the thanks, and tell the boy all about me when he is old enough to know my greatness,' replied Sheikh Abbas.

And then he shut his eyes and passed in peace away.

A moment later, as Heber knelt in prayer beside his dead father, there came Seyf, the dwarf, to tell of the third happening on that eventful night. He bent his head and salaamed to his dead master and then turned to Heber.

'This moment,' he said, 'has been born a little camel as white as the moonshine on snow! It is as if some metal-worker had fashioned a baby camel of pure silver. A most exquisite beastling and rich with promise of good fortune to the clan, for there is only one creature more blessed of heaven than a white camel, and that is a coal-black camel.'

'Would that my father had lived to hear this happy news,' answered Heber; and then there rose in the night a sound of sorrow and wailing, for the desert men lifted their voices in sad songs and the women wept to know that great Sheikh Abbas had passed away from them.

Indeed, they all wailed until the moon had sunk into the sands and another day was near. And the face of the moon as she sank was red as though she, too, wept.

Chapter II

•

The Oasis

The morning dawned very grandly out of a sky without a cloud, and suddenly along the black mountains there ran a thread of gold to tell that the sun was on his way. And presently blue smoke trickled up into the sky from a hundred camp-fires, and the people ate and talked and waited for a word of command from Sheikh Heber. He was their master now, and when morning came the old men of the tribe assembled themselves and went to the chieftain's tent. Then they lifted the spear of Sheikh Abbas, that had stood at the entrance, and set up the spear of Sheikh Heber in its place. They salaamed to their new leader and promised to serve him faithfully and do his will, even as they had followed his father before him.

CHAPTER II

'We will walk in the way that he walked,' promised Sheikh Heber, 'and strive to be as brave and wise as he. We know each other, dear people, and we love each other, and you shall find my yoke sit lightly on your shoulders and my thought be ever how to lead you to new pastures and good hunting, where men and beast shall alike be blest.'

But seeing they were now only two days' march from their oasis, Sheikh Heber bade the camp should be lifted on the morrow and the journey made, that their dead chieftain might lie with his fathers and the days of mourning be observed.

Now Heber went round the tents and received the welcome of his clan. He knew them all well and understood them; and they knew him and guessed that he would be a good leader and a kind master. But he was not like his father and not so fiery, or so swift to draw the sword. Sheikh Abbas had always held that deeds spoke louder than words, and some of his greatest successes were the result of this opinion. He was used to act first and talk afterwards, because he found it much easier and pleasanter to talk after he had gained a victory than before. He knew the hearts of men, and looked far ahead and always took care not to win a battle with his sword today and lose it with his tongue tomorrow. But the new Sheikh did not rejoice in fighting for the sake of fighting. He was a powerful Arab, well skilled in war, and could fight as well as anybody and better than most; but he had a great love of peace, and liked not to shed blood if the difficulty could be composed with a friendly talk. His instinct was to compromise, which means that he would give and take and yield a point here in exchange for an advantage somewhere else. Which was just the opposite of Sheikh Abbas, who liked to take but strongly objected to give; and when people feel so, nothing can be done about it except the miserable business of knocking the life out of each other to see which shall be top dog.

Heber had a great joy as well as a great sorrow now, for he held his baby son in his arms and looked into the little boy's eyes. The wise women of the camp told him that the infant showed great promise, and he was glad.

Presently he went with Seyf to see the other baby that had been born in the quarters of the camels, and found, indeed, that the small thing was silver bright and of perfect proportions. His mother was a lovely dromedary called Morgiana – a kindly and docile lass which Heart's Delight, Sheikh Heber's wife, always rode when the clan marched. Morgiana was no common camel, for the common camels are used for rough, heavy work, and even eaten sometimes. They carry the tents and baggage and are apt to be very grumpy and snappy if they think their loads too heavy, and they always think their loads too heavy. They give good milk and have their virtues; but the mother of the White Camel gave the best milk of all, though now she would have to keep it for her son. Another good thing the camel does is to provide beautiful wool; and if you have ever had a coat or a blanket made from it, you know how warm and soft it can be.

Camels have not got so much brains as horses, and though a horse will love its owner if he is good to it, a camel never cares much about men and only does what he is told because he must. Which is sensible of him in a way, though even then he grumbles a good deal about it.

But now a curious thing happened, for while Heber admired the baby camel, Seyf told him that here was no ordinary camel at all, but a most wonderful creature with strange and unusual powers.

'Think not,' he said, 'that you are looking at a common, everyday, young camel, only odd because it is as white as dawn. This small beast is already marked out for greatness. I dreamed wonderful dreams about him last night, and I heard his name spoken by the will of Allah, and was also told that this new-born camel must belong henceforth and for ever to your new-born son. Sense and wisdom, above all that were ever known to his race, will belong to him; his life will be in your son's hand and they will do each the other's will and guide and sustain each other in the battle of life, which all who live must fight.'

Had anybody but Seyf said these queer things, Sheikh Heber had laughed at him; but nobody ever laughed at the dwarf, because it was not good to flout the tiny man. Therefore his master listened and asked a question.

'What, then, is the camel's name if it was told you in your dream?' he said.

'He shall be called Ben Josef,' replied Seyf. 'That is his name; and your son shall be called Ali, for so I dreamed that he should be.'

'His name is for his mother to choose,' answered Heber and Seyf responded.

'Assuredly that is so; and when you ask her, your wife will tell you that Ali he shall be called.'

And Heber found the dwarf spoke true, for Heart's Delight had already determined upon her little son's name. And though nobody asked Morgiana, the mother of the baby camel, what she wanted him to be called, his name was ever Ben Josef, as the little man foretold it should be.

Sheikh Heber sent forward a messenger on a swift dromedary to the oasis, that the people might hear the news of his father's death, and then the tents were struck and the camels loaded and the flocks herded up for the journey home. Many of the live things had to be carried, but the dogs and sheep and horses went on the pad and hoof. The cats could not tramp the desert, so they travelled in baskets and slept very comfortably, and the chickens also went in baskets. Heart's Delight and her son were carried very carefully in a litter borne by trusty men, and the baby camel was also carried in a litter while his mother walked beside him. Sheikh Heber rode his father's horse beside the bier whereon Sheikh Abbas lay covered by a black canopy, and Seyf rode upon a camel and sang mournful songs. It was a sad procession, and the company took two days to reach home.

In the heart of the desert there are not many birds about, because there is little to interest them there, but now as they neared the oasis, many beautiful birds began to appear, just as when an ocean-going ship, long lonely, begins to see the great gulls and sea-fowl round her again and to know that land is near and her voyage nearly ended. Lovely and useful birds flew about the Bedouins now, and many great eagles and hawks that preyed upon the lesser things. There were partridges and quail and pigeons on the wing, and at the water-holes and small wadis lived ducks and cranes and herons. But the most precious and lovely desert bird is the hoopoe, which is not only a thing of joy in itself but a most honourable bird because it once took messages from King Solomon to the Queen of Sheba; and a bird entrusted with such important letters must be more noteworthy than most others. Ostriches sped across the desert in single file sometimes, but there was no hunting today and the great company moved steadily onward.

Long before they reached it all thoughts were turned to that glimmer of misty green where, like an emerald, their oasis shone upon the lion-coloured sands. It lay there jewelly and delicious for eyes, long weary of the eternal grey desert, to rest upon. Because green is the colour that sight of man best loves, and if you live in a town, amid grey and black and even red houses, you know how you delight to get away now and then to the woods and fields, and feast your eyes upon the bright welcome of grass and leaves spread round you.

Little by little the oasis came nearer and bulked larger upon their sight until they could see the forests of the date-palms, the verdant meadows stretched beneath them and the gleam of white huts peeping through the foliage. The oasis was rich in pure water that bubbled up from Nature's stony cisterns far below the sand. In the passing of long centuries these fountains had turned the desert dust into rich soil, where good things of every kind could grow and flourish. Every acre of the earth was precious, and the Arabs carried water from the wells so that it ran about in a silvery network and each living herb

and tree received its share. And here was the blessing of shade under the groves of the palms so that
men could move and labour, and the blaze of the sun
was tempered for them by the mighty crowns of the
trees.

Of course the grandest feature of the oasis was the
palms themselves. They are both bread and jam of
life for the Arabs, and the desert people speak of an
oasis of five hundred palms, or ten thousand palms;
so that when you know how many palms are there,
you also know about how many people live there. For
the dates are the life of the oasis and simple folk wor-
ship the date-palm, arguing that without it life must
end. Eaten ripe or stewed with butter, the date is the
people's food, and though you may be surprised to
hear it, there are no less than a hundred sorts of
date-palm – some very good, some rather poor and
stringy and tough. The very best of all comes from
the Kholas date – the King of the dates. He is two
inches long, of a clear and amber gold in colour, and
simply melts in your mouth.

The Kholas has lovelier leaves than the others, and
to skilled eyes his fern-like and dainty foliage is quite
different from the rest of the phoenix palms. These
glorious dates flourished at Sheikh Heber's oasis, but
they numbered few compared with the brown dates,
and they were kept for the Sheikh's family, or his visitors, when anybody of importance happened to call.

Now the ground grew green and soft as they came
into the outlying country of the oasis and the grass
conquered the eternal sand, so that all the camels
snorted with joy and the sheep wanted to stop and
begin to eat at once. The desert herbage thickened

and spoke of blessed water beneath, and thousands of bright scarlet anemones shone everywhere together with asphodels and other flowers. Then they came to cultivated earth and saw little fields of millet ripening, and drifts of coffee shrubs and vineyards, where white grapes and black grapes loaded the trellised boughs. For, although Allah does not allow his children to drink wine, they may eat grapes as often as they please and quench thirst with their sweetness, or pluck them and let the sun turn them into sugary raisins. And if they overdo it and eat too many, there is the senna-tree close at hand ready and willing to put them right again.

They passed by balsams, which make the most precious gum of Arabia; and the incense-trees, whose burning juice is sweet to the nose; and the henna-trees, with which the Arabs dye their clothes. There were pomegranates and figs, and apricots growing red-gold upon the bough; while beneath them flourished melons and cucumbers and lettuces and other good things; but above all and better than all, the noble date-palms clustered and wove their ferny crowns together and hung themselves with aigrettes and necklaces and streamers of dates from one year's end to another.

And, though most of the middle-aged people whom you know love their coffee better than their dates, because Arabian coffee is the best in the world, I expect you are like the Arabs themselves, and love their dates better than their coffee.

You cannot, of course, have everything perfect, and even in this lovely oasis there were troublesome creatures that chose to live there and be a nuisance to the clan. Snakes hid among the stones of the wadi, and some were harmless, but some poisonous. There were many insects that stung and bite and would not let people alone, and the scorpions were nasty customers too; but the creature most hated of all flying things was the locust, and when an evil wind blew and sent them by the million to eat up every leaf and blade of grass and ravage the growing crops, then - the outlook became very sad and serious, and the Bedouins knew that a period of hunger and thirst would soon have to be faced and fought. However, the locust is eatable, just as shrimps are eatable, and Arabs can cook him and eat him, which is the only thing to be said in his favour.

So the people entered their ancient home and brought the dead master to sleep in its shady, green loveliness for evermore.

Now followed days of mourning and solemn rites, when Sheikh Abbas was laid to rest with his fathers; and after the ceremonies were celebrated and the tears shed and the fast of sorrow kept, everybody cheered up again and felt hopeful about the future and comforted themselves with the thought that Sheikh Heber was going to be a kind and gentle ruler, keep the clan going and maintain its dignity and importance among all the neighbour clans who lived in that desert world.

Yet the oldest people, who had fought many a good fight in their time, rather hoped among themselves that the tough spirit of Sheikh Abbas would not forget them, but that he would remember his servants, breathe upon them, keep them hardy and fearless, and not suffer his son to be too gentle and easy-going. Because a Bedouin sheikh must be pretty stern and hard and stand no nonsense from other Bedouin sheikhs if he is going to be a success and make his fighting men love him and his folk trust him.

Chapter III

♦

The Adventure of Sir Brown

WHEN the baby, Ali, was brought for the first time to see the baby, Ben Josef, the little boy and the little camel both showed great delight, made much of each other and started a wonderful friendship. At first it seemed just a natural friendship between two beautiful, new-born things; but as they grew older, the sharp eyes of the dwarf discovered much more in it than just two little ones playing together. It was Seyf who found that Ali and Ben Josef actually understood each other and could talk together in a language of their own! They did not talk camel language exactly, nor yet the language of the Arabs, but before Ben Josef had mastered his own way of speech and before Ali could talk at all, they had some queer way of telling each other what they were thinking about. They were both rather lovely, for Ali had a round, brown face and shining eyes and black, shining hair that curled round his little ears, and a most delicious smile, and Ben Josef's eyes were bright and gentle and his head was covered with curls, too. But they were snow-white and very soft. Most camels have rather a tired expression and don't look very happy, as though they were always brooding over their troubles and wondering why Allah made men and women folk to worry them and keep them working so hard; but Ben Josef had a kindly, cheerful countenance, and there was a look in his eyes different from the look of other camels. He always did what Morgiana told him and was a very good son, but from the first his great interest in life turned upon Ali, and they dwelt much together and became closer friends every day.

Of course, a camel grows up far quicker than a boy, and Ben Josef's legs grew longer and longer and his silky white hump grew bigger, so that in a few years he was ready to be ridden; and the proudest day of his life was when they put a little saddle on him and set Ali on his back with Seyf, and the Sheikh's son went for his first ride. Ben Josef promised to be a very big camel and he strode along with magnificent strides. He had already been taught all that he had to know, and was so clever that he learned everything very quickly and understood by the touch of Seyf's almond switch on his side which way to turn, and by the sound of his voice whether to go faster or slower or stop altogether. It was too soon for Ali to ride alone, of course, but Ben Josef longed for the time when the dwarf would not come too, and he and Ali could go off together.

Though the boy did not grow up as quickly as the camel, he soon showed himself to be clever, with good wits and plenty of sense. He talked early, and often surprised his mother and father by saying things which showed that he was going to be bright and keen and worthy of such a fine mother and father. Seyf explained this to Heart's Delight.

'Your son,' he said, 'knows more than other children, because he understands Ben Josef; just as Ben Josef already knows more than other camels, because he understands Ali. They exchange their ideas, and Ali tells the young camel all sorts of things about people, and Ben Josef tells him all sorts of things about animals. So they share what they know and help to make each other wise.'

When he was six years old Ali began lessons with an aged man called Omar, who lived in the oasis and considered himself far the wisest person in it. He was wrinkled as an old date, and he thought that what he did not know amounted to nothing at all. But it was left for Ali and Ben Josef to discover that what he did know amounted to very little either. For, by comparing notes, they found that Sage Omar had taken everything for granted all his life; but to take things for granted is not the way to become clever, and I am afraid Omar, though he looked so fearfully wise, was not really very wonderful.

You will presently hear how Ali got on with his lessons; but for the minute we must think about Sheikh Heber and the adventures of the clan under his leadership.

CHAPTER III

Now Sheikh Abbas had been a different sort of man and looked at life in a different sort of way. Some people think that there is not much to choose between desert Bedouins and desert brigands; but Sheikh Abbas would have been very angry if anybody had said that to him, or called him a brigand. He was fierce and hard and over-mastering, and he loved a fight and taught his young men to do the same; but he had his own ideas about rightness, and his success was largely owing to the fact that once he had made up his mind he didn't change it again. He saw that Allah helped the strong, so he made his tribe as strong as he could and trained them in the use of arms and taught them that to be brave and fearless before the enemy was the thing to aim at, if you wanted to beat him. The Bedouin battles were generally about grazing-grounds, for browse is scarce in the desert, and there was great rivalry between the wandering companies for the places where their sheep and camels and horses could feed and prosper. Therefore, if Sheikh Abbas came to a favourite spot and found weaker people camped upon it for the sake of the herbage and wadis of water, he drove them away, and if they stopped to argue about it he killed a few, just to hasten the rest. He was widely known and not a little feared, but other Bedouins did not much care for him because of his harsh manners and hard heart and determination always to put his own people first.

Sheikh Abbas always said that he was a simple shepherd and that all he wanted was merely the best of everything; but he grew furious when he fell in with other simple shepherds, who wanted the best of everything too. Then he said at once that he was only a simple soldier, who had to do his duty, so if the other people seemed inclined to quarrel about it, the Sheikh called up his fighting men, who were always delighted to set to work, and ready for a row, or a raid, or a foray, or a pitched battle at any time. Pastoral life these hardy fellows found very monotonous when months passed with nothing doing, so they gladly welcomed a rumpus and a bit of fighting when the chance came. It gave the men and women something to talk about, or brag about, or sing about, or cry about, as the case might be, and brought the charm of change into their nomad lives. Because change is the life-blood in their veins and keeps them hearty and happy.

And now we have to tell of a great adventure that happened to Sheikh Heber, and showed how different he was from his father and how differently he arranged difficulties when they overtook him. Sheikh Abbas had not hesitated to hold up a caravan now and then and help himself to good things, and he had taken toll of travellers many a time when he considered himself powerful enough to do so.

But if the embassy, or caravan, had a pass from the Sultan, then no Bedouin might dare to stop them, or lay a finger on their goods. Therefore wise people always waited until the Sultan had granted his safeguard, and then they knew that the fierce Arab tribes would not molest them.

But on a day when Sheikh Heber and his clan were roaming the desert, they met a company led by one who was not wise. He was called Sir John Brown, and he came from England for two reasons. He was very rich and had made a fortune out of men's underwear. Every civilized land knew how splendid were the vests and pants manufactured by Sir John Brown, and he was very properly knighted for making such successful clothes. Yet though so clever, Sir John was not wise; and now, having flooded civilization with his lovely vests and pants, he determined to bring them to the notice of savage people also, and he planned to combine business with pleasure and go for a tour across the famous Red Desert of Arabia and carry with him samples of the famous garments. He meant to go with a caravan across the sands of the great waste and finally come out at the sea, and so have a good time and enjoy himself and also do big business when he reached Muscat on the Gulf of Oman.

That was quite all right, but this is where he made a mistake. Unfortunately he had always been a very conceited man, and his great success in life did not lessen this weakness, but only made it worse. He had not travelled in the East before, and thought that it was all plain sailing and that money would do every-thing, which had always been his experience. So when there was a good deal of delay about getting the Sultan's passport, Sir John grew angry and said that Englishmen were not used to be treated in this way and that the Sultan evidently didn't know his company. Hearing this, the Sultan, who was famous for his Oriental patience and did not much admire the English, felt that it would be a useful lesson for Sir John Brown to learn that he wasn't everybody; and so he decided to keep him wasting his time for another fortnight. Because Western people and Eastern people differ in nothing more than this: that they look upon time from opposite points of view. To the Western people time is money, as they say; to the Eastern people it is nothing at all. A Japanese artist will spend a year in carving a tiny piece of ivory as large as your thumb, and think the time well spent if he has made a perfectly beautiful thing of it.

After a few more days of waiting Sir John boiled over and started into the desert without the Sultan's passport; and this is what I mean when I tell you that he was not very wise. The people who were to form his cavalcade begged him to wait patiently; but his British blood was up. He scoffed at their alarms, declared the perils of the desert all nonsense, and told the company to trust him and fear nothing.

'Let them see my Union Jack flying above our camp,' said Sir John in his fearless fashion, 'and these hang-dog ruffians of the desert will take very good care to keep their distance.'

And when old Arabs assured him that, shameful though it might sound, there were actually people who had never seen a Union Jack, or knew its awful meaning, the gallant man simply refused to believe them.

So the caravan started, and when they called a halt at night the Union Jack was set up on a tall pole, and all went well until they came down into that region of the desert where Sheikh Heber was the great man and master. And when Sir John's party happened to be encamped near Sheikh Heber's party one night and darkness had fallen, Seyf, cruising about on his camel alone, as he often did, came upon the encampment. His eyes glittered and his mouth watered, because he saw rich stores and many camels and great chances of booty for Sheikh Heber and his clan if all went well. In fact the only thing that didn't interest him about the caravan was the Union Jack hanging from its pole in the moonlight. So Seyf alighted off his camel and made it fast and crept in among the tents to have a talk with the Arabs and hear what it was all about. They were kind to him and gave him food and drink and told him how the caravan was bound for the distant sea with rich stores of underclothing and all manner of good things; and when the dwarf asked whether they carried a Sultan's passport to make them safe, the Arabs confessed that they did not. Perhaps they might have told a story about it and pretended they had a passport if they had liked Sir John, but unfortunately he had taken rather a high hand with them and ordered them about and had not been very respectful of their manners and customs. So these Arabs didn't care in the least whether his expedition got into a mess with the Bedouins. They even rather hoped it would.

That was all Seyf wanted to know, and he returned to his camel and sped back to the clan with his good news. It was so important that he went to Sheikh Heber's tent and woke him up and told him that a wonderful caravan was crossing the desert quite close and travelling without the Sultan's protection.

'Allah has willed this good fortune,' said Seyf, 'and I should start early if I were you.'

'We want something to brighten us all up,' answered Sheikh Heber. 'You have done well, dwarf; and shall get your reward. Myself will lead the fighting men, though I am glad to think that this is not a matter for fighting. I shall talk with Sir Brown, and he will quickly understand that he has met with a slight misfortune. Let us hope he will be reasonable about it.'

Next morning Sheikh Heber mounted his glorious Arab steed, having first put on the robes of a great chief; and he rode at the head of one hundred splendid fighting men all armed with spears and long rifles, while in their belts they carried glittering knives and beautiful pistols with ebony and silver butts. They all much hoped that fighting was in store and longed to kill somebody and have a good time; but Sheikh Heber warned them that nothing of the sort was to be expected.

'Kind and friendly words are all that shall pass between us,' he said, 'for we have no quarrel with the people of this caravan, and I feel sure that it will not be necessary to kill anybody. When Sir Brown understands that he is doing wrong to invade my territory without permission, he will, of course, see that he must make good the wrong. The English are said to be very kind-hearted and great upholders of justice.'

So the warlike party rode away with Seyf to guide them, and presently they came upon the caravan, which was just preparing to make a start. Suddenly, over the ridges of the desert sand, popped up Sheikh Heber on his chestnut charger, and a moment later the fighting men thundered after them in a cloud of dust.

Sir John was outside his tent shaving his chin when the party appeared and he stared at them and shouted to a dragoman, who was his interpreter and understood English.

'What's all this? A circus?' he asked.

CHAPTER III

And the interpreter shook his head. He had expected a visit, after talking to the dwarf on the night before, and was really delighted. But he tried to look very solemn.

'No, Sir Brown,' he answered. 'This is not a circus. These are fighting Bedouins who rule this region of the Red Desert and have their lawful occasions here. They are coming to see you and learn what you may be doing in their lands.'

'Stuff and nonsense!' replied the Englishman. 'I'll talk to them. Don't they see the Union Jack?'

'They cannot fail to mark your grand flag,' replied the Arab, 'but you must explain to them why you have brought it here.'

By this time the horsemen had arrived and drawn up in a body, while Sheikh Heber came forward, called to an Arab to hold his horse, dismounted and advanced on foot into the camp.

Sir John hastened forward and his interpreter came with him. Sheikh Heber saw a little fat fellow in shorts, a khaki shirt and a big sun helmet. Sir John was very florid and his face was plump, his hair grey, his eyes bright blue. To the eyes of Sheikh Heber Sir John appeared neither beautiful nor important. He thought the knight was undersized and unusually ugly even for a white man, so he guessed that he must be a servant and of no account.

'I would wish to welcome the master and leader of this caravan,' he said to the interpreter; and when Sir John heard him, he puffed out his chest and looked fierce and formidable.

'Tell the fool that I am the big noise here,' he said, 'and ask him his business.'

So the interpreter spoke to Sheikh Heber, but he did not translate Sir John's speech very well, because he did not understand exactly what 'big noise' meant.

'This is Sir Brown, great Sheikh,' he explained. 'He is the Loud Bang here and wants to know your business.'

Then Sheikh Heber smiled and replied that his business was not the matter in hand.

'I am here to learn Sir Loud Bang's business,' he answered. 'My business is my own and does not concern him.'

The Englishman now began to see the point and spoke impatiently to the interpreter.

'Evidently they are cadgers and robbers,' he said, 'so give them a crate of bananas, or some glass beads or something, and tell them to be off. I don't want a row. We ought to be on the move.'

Sheikh Heber heard this suggestion and smiled very sweetly. 'I never have a row with anybody if I can help it,' he declared. 'I agree with Sir Loud Bang that a row is most unpleasant and as a rule quite needless. But tell him that I don't like bananas and my trusty followers hate them. Nor do we care about glass beads very much. Explain to your leader that he is trespassing, and to trespass on the land of others is a grave fault and must be paid for properly.'

When Sir John heard that he was trespassing, he grew redder than a boiled lobster and his blue eyes simply blazed with rage.

'Trespassing!' he cried, looking over the countless miles of empty sand. 'Who the (very bad word) wants to trespass on a place like this? I'm merely going across your beastly desert and getting off as quickly as I can.'

'Be calm,' begged the Sheikh. 'It will hurt your health if you get any hotter, and I should not like the great Englishman to go pop and make a mess on my desert.'

'What does the rascal want? Tell me what he wants and let us have done with him and his ragamuffins!' cried Sir John.

Then Sheikh Heber bowed low and made answer.

'My way is always to be just and fair' he said, 'and when Allah is good to me, I am good to others, as He would wish. I shall ask only for proper payment; but I must not ask too little, because that would be to undervalue the blessing that Allah has willed to bestow upon me. I am going to take ten camels out of your caravan; and they shall be laden with ten bales of merchandise from your rich stores. That would seem to be just payment for your sad intrusion.'

When Sir John heard this his face grew redder than ever and he simply danced with anger. Meantime Sheikh Heber chatted kindly and mentioned some other things that he proposed to carry away.

'My dwarf, Seyf, heard rich music in your tent last night, Sir Loud Bang,' he continued, 'and your people told him that you have a machine called a gramophone, which discourses sweet melodies and adds much to the joy of life. My wife adores music and I shall take this trifle to her with your compliments, and she will hope that some day, when you come to see my oasis, she may thank you for it.'

'Is there anything else the knave wants?' asked Sir John, who was now almost too angry to talk; and when his visitor heard the question, he jumped at it.

'Tell your lord that, since he is so good, there are several other things,' he answered. 'I see that this fine Englishman begins to know how wrong he was to trespass on my desert and is anxious to make proper amends. But I shall not press him too hard. I am called 'the Merciful' and not for nothing. So, to please him, I will take two of those fine new tents also, and other little mementoes of a pleasant meeting.'

Then the Englishman turned to his interpreter, who was much enjoying the business, and said:

'What would happen if I got my revolver and shot this scoundrel?'

Of course the interpreter knew exactly what would happen. 'If you took the life of this great sheikh, Sir Loud Bang,' he answered, 'every member of your company would be a dead man in exactly a minute and a half; and what would happen to you yourself, I haven't got the heart to tell you.'

'Can't we put up a fight, then,' cried Sir John. 'There are quite as many of us as there are of these desert rats!'

'No,' answered the interpreter. 'We are men of peace – humble carriers and servants. If any such thing were attempted, our state would soon be much worse than it is at present.'

Sir John turned to the Sheikh and pointed to the Union Jack. He was too angry to remember that Sheikh Heber could not understand him and he said.

'If you insult the British flag, you brown black-guard, you'll live to wish you had never been born!'

But Sheikh Heber only smiled and bowed and showed great pleasure.

'Since you wish me to take your flag, too, I will do so,' he said. 'I shall keep it in memory of the great Sir Loud Bang, and I shall fly it on rare occasions with my own.'

He then uttered a word of good advice:

'Let the great man now return to his tent and say "Kismet" and cool down,' he suggested. 'The sun grows hot and we must not detain his caravan any longer.'

Then, feeling that nobody loved him, poor Sir John threw up the sponge, said some more very bad words, which the interpreter fortunately could not translate, and prepared to return to his tent.

'You shall pay for this, if I'm anybody,' he threatened, and Sheikh Heber, ever courteous and kindly, made answer:

'Here, dear friend, you are rather less than nobody; but I feel sure that you must be a very famous personage in your own famous country.'

In twenty minutes the necessary exchanges were made, and Seyf, who was a great expert of camels, had chosen the ten best from the caravan and laden them with bales and bales of Sir John's celebrated underwear. He had then taken two new tents, the gramophone and a variety of other little matters, while the fighting men, to atone for their disappointment, helped themselves to various useful trifles in memory of the happy occasion.

When all was over and the force prepared to depart, Sheikh Heber told the interpreter to order Sir John before him; which he did do and the Englishman refused to come.

'Tell him to clear out and be (very bad word indeed) to him,' said the baffled knight.

But the Sheikh only shrugged his shoulders and sent half a dozen of his toughest warriors to bring Sir John along.

'I think,' he said, 'all is now as it should be and honour satisfied and your conscience clear. We are equals and, I hope, friends. And it is because I wish to show you how good a friend I can be that I am going to give you a little advice, Sir Loud Bang. First direct your people not to load that tall dromedary today. He has a bad sore upon his back and must be rested until he is well and strong. And now as to yourself, dear friend. When you leave my desert, you will enter the domain of Sheikh Khalid, who, I am sorry to say, does not share my great love of peace. I, as you have found, always seek to compromise and deal justly with my neighbour; but poor Khalid entertains very mistaken opinions on the subject of justice and causes Allah much needless sorrow. He declares that might is right; therefore, when you journey into his country without a passport, he will chastise you and smite your treasure and not feel content with a modest souvenir as I have been. And beyond Sheikh Khalid, between him and the distant sea, are other fierce and ungodly rulers who will each in turn avail themselves of your visit, so that by the time you reach the ocean, if you should ever be fortunate enough to do so, you will probably have little left beyond a pair of your own magnificent pants.'

The interpreter conveyed this warning to his master and Sheikh Heber concluded.

'Therefore I pray the great Englishman that he will

not tempt my people to do evil. I beg him to return and plead with the Sultan for a passport, so that all shall proceed safely and fruitfully without heat and hard words and broken heads.'

Then Heber mounted his charger, and it was seen that he had fastened the Union Jack to his spear, so that it fluttered bravely over the desert as he and his companions and their rich reward disappeared and the great sand swallowed them up.

That night the Sheikh sent a little present of royal dates and figs and apricots to Sir John, together with the kids of goats and a fine fowl or two; and he was very glad to hear from the messenger that Sir Loud Bang had taken his advice and started to go back. Indeed Sir John had changed his mind about his expedition altogether. He had told the interpreter that he already felt sick of Arabia and hated both the climate and the people and was going home to England at once, to put his wrongs before the Government.

Sheikh Heber sat in his tent that night and Heart's Delight played the gramophone and loved it.

'An example of how kind words are so much better than harsh deeds,' said the Sheikh. 'Loud Bang was a hideous little fellow, as red as a radish, with scantly hair and dreadful eyes as blue as the sky. And if you can think of anything uglier than blue eyes, I cannot. But he is as Allah made him, for He wills that mankind should be of every colour, and I do not quarrel with ugliness of the body. Sir Loud Bang, however, appeared to have an ugly soul also, and that is his own fault. We can all make our souls good-looking if we try hard enough.'

'Peace be with him,' answered Heart's Delight, who never said anything unkind about anybody. 'I fear he must much miss this heavenly music tonight.'

'It will teach him patience to be without a gramophone until he can go home and buy another,' said Sheikh Heber. 'Allah may will that we should lose most things; but He never wills that we should lose our temper; and if people only knew what they look like when their tempers are lost, I am sure they would take care never to lose them.'

Then Sheikh Heber lighted one of Sir Loud Bang's cigars and found it very good indeed.

Chapter IV

◆

The Adventure of the Goat

Now Ali and Ben Josef were both nearly seven years old, and the little boy worked at his lessons with Omar, and the camel was little no longer but grown up into a big, splendid fellow who towered like a beast of burnished silver over the sand, while his long, powerful legs and magnificent stride carried him and his master where they would go. He was very strong and could keep up a speed of six miles an hour for fifteen hours at a time; and he was so wonderfully made, with little cisterns inside him, that he could travel for six whole days without a drink!

But for the present, while his parents were away roaming in the desert with their people and their flocks, Ali stayed in the oasis and went on with his lessons. Seyf often stayed too, when he was feeling lazy, so the little boy had somebody to talk with who was more cheerful than old Omar, his schoolmaster. The ancient sage did not get on with Ali, and they puzzled each other, because the child had a very inquiring mind, and Allah had so made him that he always wanted to know the reason for things. But He had made old Omar differently, for what he always wanted to know was only the things themselves. He had read books for eighty years and so, of course, he knew millions of things; but he was foggy about reasons.

Seyf, the dwarf, did not like Omar and thought him rather a duffer.

'I don't believe anybody could be as wise as Sage Omar looks,' said Ali once to Seyf.

'And I should never have thought anybody could be such a fool as he really is,' answered the tiny man.

This was rude of Seyf, because Omar had spent his whole life collecting information. But he always found that Ali wanted to go back to the beginning of things which the ancient man had long ago forgotten, if indeed he ever knew them. So when Ali kept asking 'Why?' he pulled his white beard and grew snappy. He knew that what he tried to teach the little boy was true; but he couldn't remember for the life of him why it was true, or why he believed it; so he had often to tell Ali not to ask silly questions but take his word for it. And when a schoolmaster asks you to take his word for anything, then you had better ask somebody else about the matter, because if your teacher wants you to have faith in him, then it is his business to tell you the reasons for things if he knows them himself. And if he is honest and admits that now and again he doesn't know the reason any more than you do, then you will feel that he can be trusted.

'You must not waste so much time asking foolish questions,' said Omar to Ali. 'You ask so many questions that you never have time to learn anything, and at this rate you will end by being a very ignorant little Arab and knowing nothing at all.'

'But if you don't know the reasons for anything, dear Sage Omar,' answered Ali, 'why do you believe such a number of things?'

'We cannot live without faith,' answered Omar. 'The world of men turns upon faith, and if there were no faith between Allah and man, and between man and man, to believe without reasons, then the world would go down into night. And for you it is enough to know that what I teach is true, without worrying your childish brains as to why it is true.'

But Ali's brains, though still very young, were not exactly childish. He was a boy whom many schoolmasters would have found rather interesting to teach, because of his funny need for getting to the bottom of things.

For example, when they were doing simple arithmetic, Omar often despaired of him. One day the old man told his pupil that twice two were four.

'Why?' said Ali.

'Because they are four and could not be anything else,' answered Omar.

'Why are they four and not three, or five, or ten?' asked Ali.

Omar tried to be patient.

'Because it is an eternal and everlasting fact that twice two have always been four from the beginning of time and always will be to the end of time,' answered Omar.

'How do you know it is a fact?' inquired the obstinate boy. 'How do you explain it, dear Omar?'

'Explain it!' cried the old man. 'You don't want to explain it. Nobody need waste their time explaining a fact.'

'But if you can't explain it how do you know it is a fact?' asked Ali. 'Perhaps it isn't. If nobody can explain it, perhaps two and two are not four after all, dear Omar!'

Then Omar shut up the lesson-books and told Ali to be off before he got angry. And when the boy was gone, he considered him and sighed and began to fear that the Sheikh's son had a screw loose, as they say, and would never grow up to be worthy of his family or the clan.

The White Camel stayed at the oasis with Ali, but Ben Josef hoped that he and his little master would soon join the wanderers and tour the desert. Ali told him what a mess he was making with his lessons, and they talked together in their own mysterious fashion, while Ben Josef quite agreed with Ali that it was right and proper to try to reach the beginning of things.

'If a person believes something, then he should have grounds for his belief to make it strong and sure,' he said. 'Things as they are cannot be understood without knowing about things as they were, because nothing explains itself. You cannot say what may happen tomorrow unless you remember what happened yesterday. Omar is too old to remember the beginnings of things.'

They talked together every day and understood and loved each other in a very wonderful manner. Ali said they must live together all their lives and, as they had been born together, so they would die together. But Ben Josef warned him that this could not be.

'The life of a camel is thirty years,' he said, 'and the life of a man may be seventy years, or more. So I shall try to get as much into my thirty years as you, I hope, will get into your seventy, or more.'

'I shall help you,' promised Ali. 'I shall help you to get everything good that I can into your thirty years. And I shall never be happy again when you have to go.'

'Your good is mine,' answered Ben Josef; 'and my remaining years will be good years if I can make yours better than they would have been without me.'

'I am already the better for you,' said his master. 'You have taught me many things that nobody else could.'

And really Ali's two teachers at this time were Seyf and Ben Josef. Both were wise, and both were wise enough to know that their wisdom was not really quite such fine wisdom as Ali's own; for the boy said things sometimes that neither the dwarf nor the camel would have thought to say; and yet they knew that he was right.

Which brings us to the adventure of the goat. It was not a very tremendous adventure, except for the goat himself; but it led to a fine result for three other people, and it happened in this manner. There was an old billy-goat called Buz, who lived at the oasis and rather lorded it over the colony of goats. He gave himself great airs and was full of vanity and opinions, and the Arabs laughed at him and gave him a new name and called him 'Sir Loud Bang.' But Seyf hated him and never tired of worrying him and making him look silly if he could. And the great goat hated Seyf and bided his time, but fully intended to settle the dwarf some day when the chance offered. Buz was a huge black-and-yellow goat with a grizzled beard and large, lemon-coloured eyes. He strode about the camp in a very haughty fashion and, at heart, believed that he was quite as big a swell as Sheikh Heber himself. Of course he was three times as big and heavy as Seyf, but the dwarf did not fear him. The little man used to creep up behind Buz, pull his tail and insult him in many ways; and once, when he found the big fellow sound asleep under a pome-granate-bush, he fetched his paints and painted one of the goat's horns purple and the other bright green. And when Buz woke up and found his wives and chil-dren and grandchildren all standing round him roar-ing with laughter, he was furious and rushed away, and washed his beautiful horns and sulked about it for two whole weeks. And then, at last, he got his chance. The tables were turned, and this time it was Buz who found the dwarf lying fast asleep in the grass under a date-palm.

'Now,' said he, 'it is my turn and I will kill Seyf once and for all and be done with the horrid little wretch.'

So he started to kill Seyf; and would very soon have knocked the life out of him; but the dwarf's time had not yet come, and Buz failed of his great wickedness. It was a jolly near thing for Seyf all the same, and he only escaped by the skin of his teeth with the timely help of somebody else. For there came the White Camel and Ali strolling along together and when they heard the dwarf screaming bitterly, they knew that he was in trouble, and made haste. But, when they saw what was happening to him, Ben Josef strode along and lifted one huge leg like a bar of steel and kicked the goat. A tremendous kick he gave, and Buz, though so big and heavy, found himself shot into the air, flung ten yards away and dropped into a little water-course that ran close at hand. Then four things happened to Buz all at once, for he found himself hurt, angry, frightened and puzzled.

'Now why,' said he to himself; 'did Ben Josef do that? I was merely killing Seyf quietly and not interfering with him. Ben is a grass-eater like myself – almost a relation, you might say, – and we have always been very good friends; and yet, just because I am removing from the oasis the most horrid little pig in it, he goes and does this!'

Then Buz thought rather gloomily of what Seyf might do next. 'He will certainly get his knife, or his pistol, and come and kill me,' he said to himself. But then he had a bright idea.

'There is one thing you cannot do to a dead goat,' thought Buz, 'and that is kill him; so I will pretend to be quite dead, and presently, when they have gone away, come to life again and escape.'

Meantime Ali had rushed to the dwarf; set about saving him and told him that he was quite safe now. It took some time to restore Seyf; but he came to presently and Ali polished him up and spoke comforting words and brought him a drink of water. Seyf was, of course, perfectly furious with Buz, and the one thought in his mind meant that the goat must die as quickly as possible. But Ali reasoned with him and reminded him that forgiveness was better than revenge and that nothing could possibly make Buz more ashamed of himself than to be forgiven. Ali, indeed, always forgave everybody.

'Buz will never forget such a good deed as that,' he said, 'and he may live to show how grateful he is.'

But Seyf did not want Buz to live.

'He is a horrid, stuck-up old brute, who has lived too long already,' vowed the dwarf; 'and the sooner he has my knife in his wicked old heart, the better for everybody.'

So Ali saw that something must be done about it and offered to make a bargain with Seyf.

The dwarf had always very much wanted to know the secret language that Ben Josef and Ali talked together, but they had not allowed him to do so, so now Ali spoke to the White Camel, and he agreed, and Seyf heard the good news that, if he forgave Buz, he should be for evermore the friend of Ben Josef and Ali and share their secret talks.

'Then we shall be three friends instead of two,' said Ali, 'and you will know the wisdom of Ben Josef and become one of us.'

The little man, feeling that it would be a grand thing to become the friend of two such fine people, consented to forgive Buz and pardon his terrible behaviour.

'But you must really and truly forgive him,' said Ali. 'You mustn't pretend that you have forgiven him and go on hating him all the time.'

And Seyf promised; and then Ben Josef spoke and the dwarf understood him quite well, so he saw that the great delight of sharing the White Camel's ideas would be his.

'I shall know if you keep your word, Seyf;' said Ben Josef; 'and if you tell a lie about it, you will be shut out of our friendship for evermore.'

'I will forgive him at once,' promised the little man. 'The sooner the better, and I will keep my word. Where is he?'

So they went to look for Buz and soon found him lying quite still with his eyes shut in the water-course.

'Alas!' cried Seyf; 'the old goat is dead!'

But Ben Josef knew better.

'He is not dead at all,' he answered. 'I only gave him one gentle kick. He is pretending to be dead to frighten us.'

Then he called out to the goat.

'Get up, Buz, and come here. We know perfectly well that you are quite all right, and we have some very good news for you.'

So Buz rose up in fear and trembling, and when he heard that Seyf was going to forgive him and be his friend in future, he could hardly believe it. But Seyf faithfully kept his word, and as a matter of fact they became very good pals indeed. In days to come you might have often seen the dwarf taking a ride on Buz and getting him nice things to eat which were beyond the goat's power to reach.

Of course the great thing was the friendship of Ali and Ben Josef and Seyf which arose out of this adventure, and they suited one another well and each brought his cleverness to the others. They all had rather a different idea of things and exchanged their opinions and had long talks. Seyf was much older than either of them, and he brought the wisdom of age and experience; but now, at twelve years old, both Ben Josef and Ali knew a thing or two and had their own opinions. If you had heard them talking together you would have soon seen the difference between them; so you had better listen to their talk, and then you will see.

While his parents were in the desert, Ali had Sheikh Heber's garden to roam in and eat in, and one day the three friends were having a rare feed of apricots and figs and dates and grapes. So Seyf talked about fruits and how delicious they were.

'There is nothing like a fat orange warm from the kiss of the sun and plucked from the parent bough,' he said. 'To pick a Jaffa orange, shining like a ball of gold from the branch, to feel his skin warm in your hand and then to open him and find him as sweet and cool inside as an orange ice – how good! That is why boys steal oranges, so that they shall eat them straight off the tree.'

'There is a right and a wrong way to steal oranges,' said Ben Josef. 'The wrong way is to take them before they are ripe; the right way is to take them just when they are ready and bursting with juice.'

'There is truly a right and wrong way to steal fruit,' admitted Seyf. 'The right way is to steal it when nobody sees you – then your world will go on much as usual; the wrong way is to be caught stealing it, because then your world will not go on just as usual, and painful things may happen to you.'

'Those who would deny dates and pomegranates, or figs and grapes to a hungry and thirsty boy, or camel, are base fellows and deserve to be robbed, in my opinion,' declared Ben Josef. 'Only a miser or a churl would call it stealing, and such people deserve to lose their fruit. Those who never give must not be surprised if others take without asking, and it is good for such greedy people to be punished.'

'What think you, Ali?' asked Seyf.

'I think you are a very downy camel and a very downy dwarf;' replied the youngster amiably. 'Right is one thing and wrong is another thing, and to steal is wrong, no matter from whom you steal. However horrid a person may be, it is not the will of Allah that you should steal his oranges; and if you do so, you are being horrid yourself.'

Ben Josef instantly agreed with him.

'Ali tells us the truth,' he said. 'His opinion, that right is right and wrong is wrong, may be open to question, because there are a great number of things to be said about that and all depends on the point of view of what is right or wrong; but when he tells us that stealing is a bad thing, we cannot deny it.'

'If you call it stealing, it is certainly a bad thing and very wrong,' agreed Seyf; 'but of course there are quite a number of other names to call it. All depends upon the point of view, as you say. You might tell me that when we catch and eat a jerboa, or a hare, or a mountain gazelle, we are stealing from Allah, or when Ben Josef finds a patch of his favourite spurge and nibbles it up, that he is doing the same. For the beast and herb are Allah's children, even as we are.'

But Ali explained that easily enough.

'We cannot steal from Allah,' he said. 'He is the Eternal Giver and pours His gifts like the sands of the desert. There is enough for all and more than enough. Not Allah's huge bounty, but our greed and selfishness and ill-will, lead to fighting and stealing. The herb makes himself a good herb, that he may fulfil his destiny and feed the beast, and the beast makes himself a good beast, that he may justify his days on earth and help man to live and eat and be strong. It is only man who falls short of what he might do.'

'Life is more difficult for you men than for us beasts,' said Ben Josef.

'It may be,' granted Ali, 'but we have reason to help us over our difficulties, and reason is just the one gift of Allah that we men use least. Your instinct enables you and all other four-footed people to live in a much more dignified and noble manner than our reason enables us. And there is something wrong with us if we have to look to horses and camels and date-palms and coffee-bushes and the flowers of the field to learn how to behave.'

'That is going too far,' declared Ben Josef. 'There are plenty of wise men who spend their whole lives trying to teach other people how to behave; only, unfortunately, the other people won't listen to them.'

'The voice of wisdom can only be heard squeaking in times of peace,' said Seyf. 'When big things are happening and the drums roar by night and day, and men are sharpening their swords and spears and dreaming of death and glory, then these fierce voices outcry wisdom and no valiant clan has time to listen to it. We may not call it wise to want to be a hero, but what do we think of a man who says he doesn't want to be one? We should tell him to put on an apron and go and nurse the children.'

'You will have to fight some day, Ali, even as your grandfather fought,' said Ben Josef; and the young man was sorry to hear it, but he knew it must be true because, when the White Camel foretold that something would happen, it always did happen.

'I will only fight in a good cause and for right and justice and honour,' he promised; and then Seyf gave his little croaking laugh, like a bull frog in the marshes.

'When ever was it heard that men fought for anything less?' he asked. 'That is what Ben Josef meant when he said the point of view is everything. And where is the human wisdom that can reconcile points of view? You may vanquish your enemy, but you will never make him think he wasn't fighting for honour and right and justice.'

'My father says that to give and take is the whole art of living,' answered Ali, 'and that if all men understood that, then there would be no fighting in the world.'

But Seyf only laughed again.

'Had your grandfather, great Sheikh Abbas, thought so, we should not be the clan we are,' he replied.

Soon after this talk, the wanderers all came back from the desert for a rest and change, so that their flocks and herds might eat the rich meadow grass that had grown up while they were away.

Heart's Delight, Ali's mother, rejoiced to be with him again and in the cool shadows of the palms once more, for she was not as much in love with the desert as Sheikh Heber, though she would never have thought of letting him dwell in it without her.

She was very glad to be with her son and hear all the home news; but one thing happened to vex Ali's father and mother a good deal, for, when they asked after his progress and bade Sage Omar tell them how he was getting on, both felt much troubled at a bad report.

Omar told them how tiresome Ali was and what a lot of precious time he wasted asking questions that didn't matter. He said he was very, very sorry about it, but had come to the sad conclusion that Ali lacked a proper brain and would, in consequence, never be a very great success.

'He is not as ordinary young people,' said Omar, and Heart's Delight answered him.

'Of course he isn't,' she said. 'Who ever thought he was? He is Sheikh Heber's son, and the grandson of Sheikh Abbas, so how could he be like ordinary young people?'

'I will show you what I mean,' answered Omar. 'Send for him and listen to him, and then you shall see.'

It was night and the sky shone full of the starry host, so when Ali came before them, where his parents sat at the door of their house, Omar bade him attend and prepared to give him a lesson in astronomy.

The old man pointed to a red star that twinkled amid its silvery companions.

'Do you see that red star, Ali?' he asked.

CHAPTER IV

'Yes, I see it, Sage Omar,' answered Ali.

'It is called Aldebaran. It is the red Eye of the Bull, the master star in the constellation of Taurus.'

'Why is it red?' asked Ali.

'It is red because Allah willed that it should be red,' replied Omar, who often fell back on Allah when he didn't know the answer to a question.

'And why is it called Aldebaran?'

'It is called Aldebaran because the ancient Arab astronomer gave it that name,' replied Omar.

'What was their purpose in giving it that name, Sage Omar? What was the reason that they chose that particular name for it and no other?' asked Ali.

At this stage of the lesson Sheikh Heber spoke. He was a great star-gazer and very learned in the matter, and he thought well of Ali's questions, because he could answer them. In fact most people rather like questions that they can answer. It is the questions they can't answer which they think so stupid.

'Aldebaran is red, Ali,' explained his father, 'because it is a very ancient star, and as a fire will burn golden bright at first and presently sink into red embers, so this mighty sun is growing cold and his warmth becoming less. And he is called Aldebaran, because he is a follower.'

'And what does he follow, Father?' asked Ali.

'He follows that little company of golden stars we call the Pleiades,' explained Sheikh Heber. 'You see them glimmering there anigh him. They are the Sisters Seven – the daughters of Atlas, who were changed into stars.'

'Right,' said Ali. 'Now I know.'

'If you would hear their names and their stories I

can tell them to you,' continued his father; but Ali was content.

'I have learned good learning tonight,' he said. 'That will be enough to remember till tomorrow. Ben Josef is so tall that he is nearer to the stars than any of us, and he knows some good things about them too.'

Then Omar went off rather crossly, Ali retired to bed and Heart's Delight spoke to Sheikh Heber.

'The dear sage is grown so old,' she said, 'that he forgets the beginning of things, because he is so near the end of them. But our Ali wants to know about the beginnings, because he is only just beginning himself. Let him now join us in the desert and live the life of the tents, where he will learn all that becomes him to know under our eyes.'

'He shall bide here until we have made one more voyage to the Purple Mountains,' answered Heber, 'and then he shall join us henceforth and learn his future business.'

But a tremendous adventure now awaited Ali and the White Camel; for the next time that Sheikh Heber and his wife set out for the far south with their fighting men and the flocks and herds terrible news suddenly reached them from home. And it was Ali and Ben Josef who brought it.

Chapter V

◆

The Adventure of the Battle

Soon after Sheikh Heber and his great company were off again to the desert, that they might seek browse for their cattle and live in tents as usual, the dwarf, Seyf, made a dreadful discovery; but when he did so, his master and the clan were already more than a hundred miles away, in the lap of the Purple Mountains, far south of the oasis.

Seyf would often mount his camel and take food and drink and roam away into the sand for a day or two, because he liked being alone sometimes. It helped him to think, and as he grew older he rather liked thinking about things in general as well as about himself in particular.

And as he wandered towards sunset about twenty

miles from the oasis, he climbed a ridge of stony ground and suddenly perceived a big Bedouin encampment in the vale beneath. He rubbed his eyes and guessed that it must be a mirage, for mirages often happen in the desert – and I shall tell you about a beauty before long; but this was no mirage. A real camp lay in the wadi below, where Seyf had meant to spend the night by a well of sweet water among shrubs and growing things. But this was Sheikh Heber's land, and no other Bedouin people had any right to be there.

'They know he is away in the Purple Mountains,' thought the dwarf; 'and so they have dared to do this monstrous thing.'

He made his camel lie down, so that it should not be seen; and then he crept to the top of the ridge and studied the big camp beneath him. It looked like a colony of huge, black toad-stools sprung up in the valley, and there were many men moving and many horses and camels, but no women and no flocks and herds. In the midst stood the tent of the chief; and Seyf's eyes being very bright, he saw the spear of the chief standing before his tent and the chieftain's flag upon it. And then he knew that it was their next-door neighbour, Sheikh Khalid, who had done this wicked deed and marched out of his own part of the desert and calmly sat down in Sheikh Heber's desert. The clans had not clashed in open war for many years; and though Sheikh Heber did not like his neighbour ruler very much and objected to his fierce and warlike ways, he had never quarrelled with him. Now the dwarf guessed that Sheikh Khalid's spies had told him how Heber was on the march and a long way off;

and so he had ventured on to forbidden land with his army. But why? Seyf could not answer that question. He determined, however, to find out if possible, and being very brave and also very cunning, he waited till the sun was down and the stars out and darkness filled the desert. Then, when lights twinkled in the camp and the jackals began to call, he set out and presently crept on his belly among the enemy's tents, that he might hear what it was all about and why they had broken desert rules and done this dangerous thing. He was, as you know, a very tiny man, and he managed to creep along without attracting any attention in the darkness until he reached a tent wherein burned lights and from which came the grumble of men's voices. Arabs were eating their supper there and talking without fear of being overheard.

And then Seyf's blood froze in his veins and he listened to a dreadful plot.

Sheikh Khalid had planned to attack the oasis while the rightful owner was far away with his company, and four nights hence, when the moon was at the full, he and his fighting host were going to swoop down on Sheikh Heber's oasis and take it from him and fill it with the strange people of Sheikh Khalid. It would be fortified and made ready to resist the returning clan, and so Sheikh Heber must surely find himself defeated and very likely killed when he came back to do battle for his own. Everything had been thought out, and the dwarf heard how the oasis was going to be taken and made strong against Heber and his people. The guard, always left there to defend it against robbers, would be slain and Sheikh Khalid's conquering forces all ready to fall upon the returning company and surprise them and defeat them and make hard terms with them and banish them from their oasis for evermore.

The dwarf gasped at this fearful news, but he kept his nerve, remembered everything that he had heard and presently wriggled away as he had come, got clear of the tents, stood up again and took to his heels like a frightened rabbit. He was soon back beside his camel, and he mounted quickly and set off at a fast trot for home. Dawn had not yet broken when he returned, and while he rode he considered the horrible threat that now hung over the clan and felt very thankful that Allah had led him to the wadi that evening and allowed him to hear what was going to happen.

Of course the thing to do would be to prevent its happening; but Seyf felt the problem was much too great for him to tackle single-handed, and when he reached the oasis safely, he called up Ali and Ben Josef; who had both gone to sleep long ago. But he roused them and told them the news and they very soon decided what must be done.

'We have four days until full moon,' said Ali. 'That is the great thing. My father is now at the Purple Mountains, and the first point to know is how far off they are.'

'They are one hundred and seventeen miles from us as the bee flies,' said Ben Josef.

'And how long will it take you, with me upon your back, to go one hundred and seventeen miles?' asked Ali.

'Exactly eighteen hours if Allah wills,' answered Ben Josef.

'Then the sooner we start the better,' decided Ali. 'You are way-wise. It is one of your great gifts never to be lost in the desert and you will be able to make a bee-line to my fathers camp. If, therefore, we start at the first grey of dawn, we shall reach Sheikh Heber soon after dark tomorrow, and that will give him time to make forced marches and be here with the fighters to defend the oasis when Khalid falls upon it.'

'The first thing is to let Sheikh Heber know what the full moon is to bring,' said Seyf; 'Once he knows, then the plans of battle will be in his hands.'

So, when the first tremor of light touched the darkness, and long before the sun burned like a huge fire over the rim of the desert, Ben Josef and Ali were off on their tremendous journey.

At first the White Camel seemed to be going rather slowly to the boy upon his back; but it was not so in truth, for Ben Josef knew what a hundred and seventeen miles was going to mean and exactly how many times his four mighty legs would have to rise and fall again before the miles were told.

The Red Desert of Dahna is far from flat. The surface rolls like a sea of enormous waves made of sand instead of water. Great tempests of wind have raised them up, and lesser winds have blown backward and forward across them so that they look as tumbled and rough as a real, stormy sea, though they lie so still.

And Ben Josef, as he rose over one ridge, sank down and rose again to the crest of the next, looked like a little, dainty, silver ship riding those mighty waves, and holding a straight, lonely course through that ocean of sand.

Boy and camel talked together while they jogged

along and the sun rose, climbed swiftly and shortened their shadows as he ascended.

'The great thing is to know what we want,' said
Ali; and Ben Josef answered,

'No, the great thing to know is how to get it. We
know what we want well enough; but Sheikh Heber
will know how to get it. He is a man of peace; but
nobody can fight better than a man of peace when he
is properly roused and feels that justice must needs
be fought for. It may be that all good things demand
to be fought for and nothing that comes for nothing
is any worth. But your father will know exactly how
to act in this matter.'

'Why do the Arabs think there are demons and bad
spirits in the Red Desert?' asked Ali. 'Is it true, or
false?'

'It is false,' answered Ben Josef 'The Arabs echo
what their mothers and fathers have told them; but
the only real danger are thirst and hunger and
simoom.'

Ali was anxious and somewhat cast down. He very
seldom felt unhappy, but this evil news had troubled
him and his spirit grew sad. Such dreadful things to
come made him take a gloomy view of life for the
moment.

'Men are not all they ought to be,' said Ben Josef,
'but you may live to see them better.'

'Camels are not all they ought to be either,'
answered Ali; 'nobody is.'

'Yes,' replied Ben Josef 'Camels are all they ought
to be, and you must not say that. Camels are wonderful – much greater-hearted and far nobler than
men think them. I only know one right-down failure

of a camel, and that's myself. I have been spoiled by too much kindness.'

'You are not spoiled at all,' answered Ali. 'Nothing could spoil you; but the case is very much sadder with me. Allah must be sick of hearing me begging to be forgiven. I am always at it.'

'Do not despair,' answered Ben Josef. 'Allah can forgive worse things than you are ever likely to do. Let us not be foolish about ourselves. We are quite all right really and doing the best we know how to do.'

So they cheered each other up and then fell silent for an hour, while the sun climbed to his topmost throne and there was no sound but the steady, endless thump of the White Camel's mighty pads upon the sand.

Clump - clump - clump - clump - clump - clump - clump - clump he went, with his great neck stretched forward, his nostrils wide open and his brown eyes fixed on the far distant horizon. And Ali seemed as part of him, squatting on his little saddle aloft and jogging up and down as Ben Josef swept along.

Then there came a surprise for far away, yet near enough to mark, there suddenly glimmered white minarets and the crowns of a thousand date-palms, while at their feet the trees and buildings were reflected in the misty face of a lake. Exquisite beauty marked this vision of still waters and the snowy towers mirrored upon them, but Ali was alarmed and feared a grave mishap.

'Alas, Ben Josef!' he cried. 'You are not way-wise after all, for you have brought us to a great oasis and there is no such thing upon our journey to my father.'

But the White Camel quieted his fears and told him what he saw.

'These are not real trees and waters,' he said. 'We are looking at a mirage – a wondrous trick of the great sun, who will lift and throw images from real things afar off into the bosom of the desert for eyes to see. You gaze upon what is as unreal in its reality as a rainbow – a gleam of promise and loveliness flung here to gladden the sight, yet lacking any promise for the heart. But even so it is good, because it is beautiful.'

And Ali understood quickly, for he always understood Ben Josef.

They halted presently in the shadow of a great rock when the mirage had vanished, and while the boy ate and drank and the camel nibbled a scrap of his favourite spurge, Ali spoke of the wonder they had seen.

'In one of Sage Omar's books,' he said, 'I have read about a sort of people called artists, who carve stones into the shape of men and beasts, and who write stories, make music, paint pictures and sing noble songs. They see things that are real to them which others do not see; they dream dreams and tell them again as best they can, and they spend their lives in trying to make better bread than is made of wheat. Surely they live in a land of mirage among fair visions that are only real to them but have no truth for other people?'

'Life itself is a mirage,' said Ben Josef; 'and every man makes his own mirages and sees in his thoughts what he would love to welcome in reality. And the greatest artists are those who have the power to make their dreams come true, so that others can share in their beauty. But the greatest of all would tell you that they lack the power to make their mirages come true, though they go on trying and trying as long as life is in them.'

'I should like to be such a man and strive to make things,' said Ali.

'It may happen,' answered Ben Josef; 'for I have known you to dream good dreams and find beauty where none but yourself thought to look for it; but just at present the future, both for you and me, is doubtful, and our time may soon end. It will all depend on what happens to us after the moon is full.'

When they were up and striding along again, Ali asked his friend what he had meant by this speech and Ben Josef explained.

'There will be fierce fighting at the full of the moon, if not before,' he said. 'When and how the battle is to be fought Sheikh Heber will decide; but battle there must be, and though you are young to fight, the craft of killing is part of your birthright and your father may feel that you cannot begin too soon. Sheikh Khalid is unfortunately not a mirage, but a solid and ferocious person who will take some very hard knocks before we get him and his fighting men under. Your father may of course forbid you to fight, and I hope he will; but as for me, I am far the largest and strongest of all the camels and I shall most certainly fight to the best of my great powers.'

'If you fight, then I shall fight with you,' said Ali, 'and if we die together it is well and much sorrow will be spared me.'

'It will be better still if we live together,' replied Ben Josef. 'And why not?'

The sun was dipping beneath the desert and,

refreshed by the twilight, Ben increased his pace. He had now travelled eighty miles but felt no weariness. Darkness came quickly and the stars told the great camel that he had not erred a span out of his way. And then, faint and far off through the night, they saw a rugged ridge lying low athwart the skyline and knew that the Purple Mountains were no more than ten miles off. As they sank in the endless trough of the sand, the hills vanished; and when they rose again to another ridge, they reappeared, growing closer and higher every minute. And so at last they came to the encampment of Sheikh Heber and filled all men there with surprise.

Ben Josef had taken precisely the time that he meant to take, and now he was fed and watered and praised. Then he tucked his great legs under him, heaved a mighty sigh of contentment and went to sleep at once, leaving the men-folk to decide what was going to happen in the morning.

Ali, too, had a good meal, but he could not go to sleep until he had told his tremendous news; and then Heart's Delight, forgetting all about what had brought him, just revelled in the joy of knowing that he was close to her, made much of him and felt proud that her son had done such a brave deed and taken this great journey all alone. But Ali only had time to eat and drink and tell his errand; for then he fell dead asleep and was carried to his father's tent and laid to rest.

Meanwhile Sheikh Heber called his captains and counsellors around him and ordered pots and pots of coffee to be made and invited all those to smoke who wished to do so. Then, when they were assembled, he told them the thing that had happened, and they listened to every word and their dark eyes flashed with rage and fury. But they kept quite calm and silent and heeded the chief's words.

'Much to my sorrow,' he began, 'I have at last had my fears of Sheikh Khalid proved only too just. I put them away from me again and again, being a man who better loves peace and a fair bargain than war and robbery; but our neighbour has now planned a deed against which words are vain and any bargain impossible. He seeks to take without giving in exchange, and since he knows that his purpose is evil, he is going about it in a most disgraceful fashion and ignoring the rules and regulations that govern fighting between gentlemen.'

'Nowadays,' said an old Arab, 'the rules and regulations are not respected. Surprise is often the secret of success.'

'So Sheikh Khalid doubtless imagines,' replied Heber, 'and I trust he may live to find the truth of it, for now, thanks to this grand run of the White Camel and my courageous son, the surprise is going to be our enemies', and not ours, as he intended.'

They were then told how Khalid had already brought his army on to Heber's land and lay but twenty miles away from the oasis.

'The bad fellow doubtless knows that we are here, more than a hundred miles distant, dreaming no evil about him,' continued their chief; 'and he is going to march upon our oasis at full moon and have it all his own way. Then, when presently we return, he will have the place fortified against us and his army ready to destroy us. That is Sheikh Khalid's abominable plot; and now we must consider our own.'

Then the captains and the wise ones all said their say and Heber listened carefully to every one. For the most part they agreed that an instant return must be made to the oasis by forced marches, so that the fighting men could prepare and fortify their home against this coming attack. They said that the flocks and herds must be left with the women and children and shepherds and old men; but the fighters on their horses and camels must start at the first possible moment. Three long marches must be needful, and then Sheikh Heber would be back just as the full moon rose. Already the company cried out to start and so make good progress before the sun was over the mountains, for by night their beasts would travel more quickly than in the glare and heat of day.

But Sheikh Heber proved more wise than any of them, for he was not the son of Sheikh Abbas for nothing, and though he disliked fighting, he had seen plenty and knew all there was to know about it.

'Your brilliant ideas fill me with admiration,' he said, 'and I am proud to have so much valour and wisdom collected in my tent at one time. You are splendid fellows and with such leaders our forces cannot fail. But, by your leave, I venture to submit another plan, which may work out better when presently we come to blows. I strongly object to the idea of Sheikh Khalid going any nearer to my oasis. He is quite near enough and the thought of his army trampling our green grass and fouling our watercourses is very painful to me. Such things would certainly happen if we prepare to defend it from inside. That we should conquer and drive off these people and take righteous toll of them afterwards is no doubt most probable, since right is on our side and right and Allah are one; but, before our victory, a great deal of mess would be made and property destroyed and many very unpleasant things happen.

'Therefore,' continued Sheikh Heber, 'we will march – not home – but to the encampment of Sheikh Khalid and fall upon him with all our might in the desert. We shall burst upon his rear just when he is happily setting out for the oasis, and thus the mistaken man will find how true it is that nothing happens but the unexpected. His spies and watchmen will all be forward upon the way to the oasis, so coming stealthily and swiftly from behind, we shall, I hope, be on top of him before he knows it and win a great victory with as little loss of precious life as possible.'

Then his people applauded Sheikh Heber, and nobody any longer felt any doubt that he was a good soldier and knew his business well. Seyf had explained to Ali exactly where the enemy's camp lay, so Heber, fetching out a map of his country, was able to set a mark on the spot and study the nearest way to get there from the Purple Mountains. The distance by a direct route was about eighty miles and Sheikh Heber decreed that his army should make two marches and fall upon Sheikh Khalid at the end of the second march.

'We must, of course, be discovered before we pounce upon them,' said Heber, 'for they will hear us, but up to the last moment they will not guess who we are in the darkness of night, and even if they do, it will be too late to get their line of battle ready before we are upon them.'

Time was all precious, but Heber bade every man

go to his tent and sleep till the watch should rouse them at the first grey of dawn. Then he, too, retired and slept soundly for three hours. He felt no fear of the coming struggle, but was sorry for one thing above all others. He knew that Ali was going to fight and that Heart's Delight would feel very sad. But the son of a Bedouin chief must do as becomes his high office and set a proper example; therefore, Ali was bound to take his place in the battle line.

Heber and his boy were up first of the whole camp, and his father talked to Ali and found him fearless and anxious to play his part.

'I am sorry for us,' said the Sheikh, 'but I am sorrier still for Khalid, because he is making a great mistake and losing his friends if not his life. This incursion will be a bad mark against him if he lives, and a dishonour to his name if he dies. He has created a lawless company who forget the rules of the game. But, as a sage has well said, "A body of men holding themselves accountable to nobody, ought not to be trusted by anybody," and whatever happens it will be exceedingly difficult for me to trust Sheikh Khalid any more.'

Heart's Delight was very brave about Ali going to battle, because she knew it would be quite useless to make a fuss. If you marry a Sheikh, you must behave accordingly, so she kissed Ali and said, 'Allah be with you while we are absent one from another.'

And that was all.

No fear for the safety of the camp existed, and it was left with the shepherds and old people when Heber and one hundred and seventy-five mounted men set forth upon their war-like journey. Sheikh

Heber on his charger led the horsemen and Ali on the White Camel led the camel corps. They made good progress and longed to meet the enemy.

'There will probably be more of them than of us,' said Heber, 'but we shall have surprise on our side and strike the first blow, which is often the best blow.'

At noon, upon a ridge a mile ahead of the army, their leader saw a spy perched on a camel, and the distant spy saw him and instantly fled. But it was very important that the spy should not get back to Sheikh Khalid and give him warning, so two splendid riders on Arab steeds gave chase. The spy rode a big camel, and at first it looked as though they would never catch him, but a horse can gallop faster than a camel can run and they gained steadily upon him. For three hours they pursued the spy, and when they were near, he stopped his camel and fired his gun at them. But he missed and had not time to load his gun again. So he died and they took the camel, which was very tired, and went back to their army.

They camped that night after going fifty miles, which was a good day's work, and they were up and off again next morning. They had a long way to go yet, but wanted to keep fresh for the battle which Sheikh Heber knew would begin on the following night. They kept a sharp look-out for spies, but a few hours before they were due at the camp of the enemy, one of Khalid's scouts did see them and got back with the news that an armed force was on the march not far off.

Sheikh Khalid, who was giving his army a final rest before they marched to take the oasis, felt doubtful if the approaching warriors belonged to Heber; but he guessed that they did and wondered how they had learned what he was up to. However, he made hasty preparations and called his men to arms so that they might be ready if trouble was at hand. They rather doubted their spy and believed that he had only seen the mirage of an army. However, soon after sundown and in the great desert silence, the sounds of a galloping host were heard, and Sheikh Khalid had barely time to get his soldiers into battle order, with their camels and horses turned to the oncoming foe, when Heber leapt upon them like a tiger out of the night, and that tremendous battle began.

The moon rose upon it presently. She was now but one day short of full, and so bright that the battle could be carried on by her light. Mighty deeds were done and many brave Arabs on both sides fell and died in that bitter struggle. Neither party gave any quarter, for the Bedouins do not take prisoners, and all fought to kill or be killed.

Ben Josef led the camels with Ali perched upon his back, and the way he thundered down among the enemies' camels and bit them and hurled them into the dust was terrific to see. Nothing could stand against him, and though he was wounded with spears upon his breast and flanks, he made light of it and battled furiously, moving like a huge white ghost among the brown camels and leading on his friends and battering down his enemies, so that Khalid's men were frightened and cried out.

'This is no camel, but a demon,' they said. 'Heber has a devil camel fighting for him, and mortal man cannot conquer the forces of darkness!'

CHAPTER V

Meantime Sheikh Heber had striven to find his
chief enemy and slay him; but Khalid looked after
himself and escaped for a season. He fought bravely
enough, yet presently began to see that things were
not going very well with his army. He galloped here
and there and slew good men and put courage into
his force, but the tide of battle flowed steadily
against him and presently cold fear touched his heart
and he knew that he was going to lose. Defeat meant
certain death for Khalid, and there were many good
reasons why he did not want to die.

Then Sheikh Heber spied him out, and knowing
that when Khalid bit the dust the battle would be
over, he made a great effort to reach him; but Khalid
fell back and hid behind his horsemen. And that was
his undoing. For Ben Josef, after battering right
through the enemies' camels and killing three and
flinging many to the ground, turned again and
charged furiously upon them once more. This he did
three times, and Ali from his perch directed him and
helped him. And now, retreating before Heber,
Sheikh Khalid came close to the camels of the enemy
and before he knew it, Ben Josef was upon him and
overturned his steed and crashed him down upon the
sand. In another moment a dozen bitter bright lances
would have pierced the Sheik's body, but Ali cried out
to the camel men to spare his life and, before Khalid
could get free of his fallen steed, Ben Josef set a
mighty foot upon him and held him fast and made
him a prisoner.

Sheikh Khalid fought desperately to rise, but he
was powerless, and when he saw the great White
Camel towering above him with with only an

unarmed lad upon his back, he believed that his army was right and that some mighty spirit from the desert fought for Heber. So they bound him with ropes and let him live until his fate should be determined.

And looking back upon that savage night in time to come, Ali often thought what a wonderful thing it was and what a difference it had made to his whole life when he stayed the spears and suffered that wicked Sheikh to live.

Now came the turning-point of the battle, for when they saw Khalid down in the midst of the enemies camels, with Ben Josef above him, the Bedouins naturally believed their leader was dead, and that if they tarried the demon thing would slay them also.

So their courage failed, and a panic terror ran through them, and such as were still mounted and able to do so fled away into the desert, while Heber's victorious horsemen chased them and slew all they overtook.

It was a glorious victory fought against odds; and of Sheikh Heber's men twenty-five perished and thirty received wounds; but of Khalid's men fifty-one perished.

All men marvelled at what the White Camel had done to help his side and counted it a great mystery that one, so mild and gentle as Ben Josef was wont to be, should have blazed into such tremendous fighting fury and proved so terrible in war. For not only did he fight magnificently and triumphantly himself: he acted like magic upon the other camels and made them far more brave and formidable than they would have been without him. But there is a reason for everything and, in time to come, Ali learned the secret of Ben Josef's fighting genius. Ben did not know the secret himself, however, and when Ali tended his wounds and all the fighting men told him he was a great hero, he only said that he had been quite as much surprised as anybody to find what he could do in a battle.

'I hate fighting,' he told Ali, 'yet none the less I was called to fight and rather enjoyed it while it lasted. But I hope it may never happen again, because I do not like conquering and killing things. It is nasty work.'

Sheikh Heber had received one small sword wound, but it was not serious and he thought nothing of it. He rejoiced even above the joy of victory to know that Ali had suffered no harm whatever, thought the boy was rather sore from bumping up and down on Ben Josef in the battle. But he had seen war and death and was so much the wiser. As for Sheikh Khalid, his victor made him fast and, when morning came, carried him along to the oasis.

'I will decide in what manner he shall die presently,' said Heber. 'His wickedness has sent many good men to their graves and, in war, those who make war too often come off free. Only the soldiers die, not the statesmen whose craft has slain them. But Khalid is soldier and statesman both and a great chief – also a great sinner – so we must see that his punishment is worthy of his crimes.'

Then they praised Allah for giving them the victory, and buried the dead men and beasts and took what they pleased from the defeated camp and so marched to the oasis.

'We will rest two days,' said Heber, 'and dispose of Sheikh Khalid; and then we shall return to the Purple

Mountains with our good news, that we may rejoice Heart's Delight and comfort the widows and children of the fallen.

'Blessed be those who fall for freedom and honour,' he added, 'for though they are now dead, their cause is living and triumphant, their name the music of their people.'

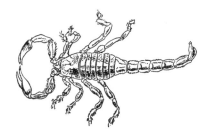

Chapter VI

◆

The Adventure of Sheikh Khalid

WHEN the people of the oasis learned of their escape and the terrible danger that had come so near them, they did two things. They made a great fuss over Seyf, who had saved them by discovering the plot just in time, and they felt the passion of the weak when the strong are conquered, and longed to watch Sheikh Khalid die. But their chief was not going to turn his enemy's death into a circus, and when the old men begged him to make a fearful example of Sheikh Khalid and suggested all sorts of horrid ways to do so, he answered, 'Only a fool tries to please everybody; but the wise man tries to please his conscience, which matters most to him.'

So, when morning came and two swift camel-riders

had set off to the Purple Mountains, to tell Heart's Delight of the victory and that all was well with her husband and son, Sheikh Heber directed that his prisoner should have a good breakfast and then be brought before him to receive a fair trial and proper sentence. Around Heber stood the old men of the clan, and beside him sat his son. Seyf was also at the trial; but Ben Josef, after his great fight, needed a long sleep, and Ali had dressed his wounds while he still slumbered and told the camel men that he must not be awakened.

Then Sheikh Khalid, who was much surprised to find himself still alive, spoke to his conqueror.

'That you have willed thus far to keep me in the land of the living,' he said, 'is a misfortune for one reason and a blessing for another. It is a misfortune, because according to the usual way of war, I should have fallen with my brave companions and paid the loser's price as they did. But it is also a blessing, because you can now hear what I should wish to tell you and do good for evil and pay me a victor's generous service before I die.'

'It will give me no pleasure to destroy you, Khalid,' replied Sheikh Heber, 'and it gave me no pleasure to destroy your brave warriors, or see my own destroyed. There would seem to be only one possible answer to your act of treachery and wickedness to a good neighbour, who has lived in peace and friendship with you for so many years.'

'I know it, Heber,' answered the prisoner. 'I am well aware that death is my portion. I have always said that the people to be killed by war are those who make war, and I have been sorry to see the statesmen and leaders and plotters, who make wars, pay no price for their villainy. But it was I who both plotted this war and fought in it, and I deserve to die a double death, so if you can think of a way to kill me twice, I shall thoroughly deserve it.

'I am not going to make any excuses for myself,' continued the fallen sheikh. 'I had long coveted your oasis and thought how much I should like it for my own. Our desert clans, just as the great nations and kingdoms of the earth, are always coveting something they haven't got, and the mighty empires of the world are those which have succeeded best in getting a grip on the property of their fellow-men. Had I stolen your oasis it would have been a very fine thing for my people, just as it was a fine thing for your people when the grandfather of the great Sheik Abbas first found it and took it for his own and made it the splendid place that it now is. But my plot has failed, and I am ready and willing to pay the price.'

'You never stopped to consider the price first?' asked Sheikh Heber.

'No,' replied his fallen foe. 'All I wanted to do was to steal your oasis; and I planned the capture to take place while you were far away. It looked to me a brilliant piece of plunder and I could not see how it was possible to fail. But Allah took your side, so all is said as to that.'

'And what more do you want to say?' asked Heber. 'I may tell you at once that you need fear no indignity in death. You are a great leader, though a wicked one, and, as a sheikh, will pass out of life with all proper respect.'

'Thank you,' replied Khalid. 'That is a generous

thing to grant me, and greatly to your credit. I do not, however, deserve it, and if it will give your people any pleasure to – however, we can leave that. I am now availing myself of your patience to ask a boon-not for myself; but my children. You can only refuse it; yet in truth not my life alone is in your hands. It is for you to say whether my son and daughter shall perish also.'

'I have nothing to do with your family,' replied Heber. 'They did not make war upon me.'

'The sin of their father will most certainly be visited on his children if you do not intervene,' explained Khalid. 'My wife is dead and I have a son of eleven years old and a daughter of twelve years old.'

'There will be wise ones in your clan to cherish them and bring your son up in the way he should go,' answered Heber; 'and I can only hope that they will teach him a better way than your own.'

'Unhappily it is not so,' replied the captive. 'My younger brother, Hassan, will take command when it is known that I am dead. And, since he has long yearned to fill my shoes and become a sheikh, he will now set about it. He has sons also, and they are tough lads who love not me, nor yet my boy and girl. The moment that it is known I am gone, my children's lives will hang upon a thread, and some day soon they will vanish from the camp like fallen flowers, while the people will be told that evil beasts have devoured them. Then Hassan and his sons will reign over the clan.'

Heber listened very patiently to this state of things, though only one other who listened was also patient. The old, wise ones didn't care a straw about

Khalid's family, and most of them felt that it would be a very good thing if his son and daughter were dispatched as well as himself.

But Sheikh Heber thought otherwise.

'You truly remark that empire is built on conquest,' he answered; 'but the greatness of an empire does not lie in vast possessions, or far-flung might of arms. It is the spirit of the empire by which it must live and endure and shine; but if that spirit is base, the empire will surely crumble and vanish. I seek to rule my little kingdom in a spirit of humanity, Sheikh Khalid, and humanity embraces all things and all people. Therefore it embraces your little son and daughter. But what would you have me do on their behalf?'

'May Allah pardon me for making war on such a man as you are,' replied Khalid, 'though I do not see how He can be expected to pardon me. As to my children, I would pray you to send messengers to my people and order the boy and girl to be given up to them and brought to you. If that is done, my brother, Hassan, who is, if possible, a bigger ruffian than I am myself, will of course be sure that you are going to kill them and save him the trouble of doing so.'

'Was he at our battle yesterday?' asked Ali.

'No,' replied Khalid. 'Hassan is the sort of man who prefers that other people should do the fighting while he does the plotting in his tent and gets the praise afterwards.'

Then Ali stood up and asked his father if he might speak, and Heber allowed him to do so.

'Since you are man enough to fight, you are man enough to talk,' he said.

But Ali made some very startling suggestions. They pleased his father and they astounded Sheikh Khalid, who could not believe his ears when he heard them; but nobody else liked Ali's ideas, and the old men shook their heads and frowned at him.

'A live Arab may be an enemy, or he may be a friend,' began Ali. 'A live Arab may be an enemy today and a friend tomorrow. But a dead Arab is no use to anybody and can no longer walk among men for good or evil.'

'We should not speak of Sheikh Khalid as a live man,' said an old statesman. 'His death is sure.'

But Ali made answer.

'Until a man is dead, he continues to be alive, and we must think of the world with Sheikh Khalid still in it.'

Then he turned to the prisoner and asked a curious question.

'What would happen if you went back to your people, great Sheikh?' he inquired.

There was a hum of indignation at such an idea, and the wise ones told Sheikh Heber to bid Ali be silent; but the boy's father refused.

'He has fought as a man and he has a right to his opinions,' he told them; while Khalid stared at Ali and for a long time felt too surprised to make any reply. At last he spoke.

'If I went back to my people,' he answered, 'my children would be safe and their enemies would be powerless; but that is a vain question, because, as yonder old man has told you, I cannot be thought about any longer as in the land of the living.'

'One does not let a scorpion sting us twice,' cried out Seyf. 'Why should you live?'

Chapter VI

'I have already accepted my death as right and just, little man,' answered Sheikh Khalid. 'I have said farewell to life and am now only thinking of my boy and girl.'

Then Heber spoke. He had been much impressed by what his son had said, and though Ali did not dare to beg for the life of the enemy, his father knew that was what he wanted. So he addressed the boy.

'Why should you wish your father's bitter foe to live, Ali?' he asked.

'That he may turn into my father's friend,' replied Ali. 'Such an act of forgiveness would not only make Sheikh Khalid an undying friend; it would do much more than that. If you forgave him and suffered him to live and go back to his people and lead his clan as of old, he would return to them a different man. The things that happen to us make or mar our hearts, and before such a deed as that the heart of Sheikh Khalid would be clean again and he would know in life what he can never know in death: the nature of the man he has tried so hard to wrong. So much for him; and for you, my father, to forgive him would make your heart sweet and clean also, for the act of forgiveness blesses both sides – the forgiven and the forgiver.'

So Ali preached his great belief in forgiveness. But the elder statesmen started up and began to chatter and protest with all their powers. They were terribly in earnest and most honest old men; so they cried out with all their might against the folly and weakness of sparing Sheikh Khalid and giving him another chance.

One after another spoke, and all begged for Sheikh Khalid's death. They argued that once a traitor, always a traitor, and declared that a man could no more change his heart than a wolf or a tiger can change his hair. They said that to pardon such a wicked enemy would be to flout Allah, Who had given him into their hands. Therefore they implored that Khalid should die, and pointed out that the Sheikh himself was perfectly reasonable and had never suggested living any longer after his defeat.

'The best that you can do, to show your magnificent generosity, is to send for his boy and girl and let them enter our camp and belong to us,' said Seyf. 'To allow this villain to return to his own people would be utter madness, and a time would soon come to find us repenting in sackcloth and ashes.'

Then a very crafty counsellor spoke out of his bitter heart. 'Forgiveness itself is an insult as often as not,' he said. 'Sheikh Khalid is a very proud man. To be forgiven would add shame and scorn to his failure and he would never cease from plotting to do you evil till he had wiped out such contempt in your blood, Sheikh Heber.'

'What say you to that?' inquired Heber, and Khalid made answer.

'It is difficult to plead and idle to promise,' he said, 'and it would be still more difficult for you, or your people, to believe me if I did either. I have never asked for favours until this hour and, as you know, the favour I do ask is for my children. If, out of your great victory, you can grant that favour and let the boy and girl come to you and grow up with your people in safety and security, then you have done a very noble thing and more than I had right to ask. I could say much and speak fair words and utter fair promises; but, seeing what I have plotted and striven to do against you, it were vain to suppose that you would believe me.'

'But if you are set free and allowed to go on living, what would you promise to do?' asked Sheikh Heber.

The captive was in no hurry to reply and thought silently before he spoke.

'The word of a broken man is but wind,' he answered, 'and I am not going to beg to live. I had already bade goodbye to the difficult business of living. But, if you command that I shall live, I only pray to Allah that He may give me a chance to do things instead of promise to do them. Words are dead until translated into deeds. The worldly wisdom of your old men is against you if you spare me; the voice of a child alone is raised upon my side. But think and think again, Sheikh Heber, before you listen to your son and ignore your statesmen.'

Heber rather liked this speech. It sounded honest, and there was that about the rough and rugged Khalid which made him feel not unfriendly.

'Can a false enemy turn into a true friend?' he asked.

'I was not a false enemy,' answered Khalid. 'I was an open enemy. In war one's plots are of course a secret, but I loved you not and wanted your oasis far more than I wanted your friendship.'

'You will not want my oasis if I choose to spare you and let you return to your people?' asked Heber.

'If you choose to spare me and let me return to my people,' replied Khalid calmly, 'I should tell them how I had met one nearer to Allah than any man I ever did meet, and I should henceforth be your comrade in happiness or grief and count your welfare as my own welfare so long as I live. That is all I have to say – only words; but words that will burn with life in my heart as the seed burns with life in the earth, until the time comes to turn them into actions.'

Then he spoke to the bitter old fellow who had said that forgiveness was an insult.

'Forgiveness may be an insult and a sign of contempt,' he said. 'But not when it comes to you with your life in its hands. To give me my life is far more than forgiveness; it is mercy, and never was mercy an insult to any man. To live, when you had already lifted the Cup of Death to your lips, may be a disappointment and misfortune, but not in my case. To live now would be as though the sand-foundered Arab has seen a mirage laughing at him over the desert and Allah had turned the mirage into reality and saved the wanderer and brought him back to life after he thought all was lost.'

Then Sheikh Heber spoke and forgave Sheikh Khalid.

'I pardon you and trust you,' he said, 'and for the peace of your people and your children, it is well that you should not delay to return to them.'

'May you live to see and may I live to show the answer to that,' replied Khalid.

Then the people went away shaking their heads and saying that Allah had made Heber go mad; and the two sheikhs ate salt and broke bread together. Khalid was soon mounted upon an Arab steed, and he blessed the camp of Heber and departed; but, before he did so, Ali gave him two little gifts for his boy and girl, and Sheikh Khalid took the gifts and promised to deliver them.

'I have come back to life by a short cut,' he said, 'and am still as a man roused from wonderful dreams; but I shall soon awaken.'

When Ali told these things to the White Camel, Ben Josef took his side and said that all would be well.

'Such things do not happen by chance,' he declared, 'and a time is coming when you will be rewarded for this day's work and your father also. Yet the greatest reward of all will come to you.'

'What will it be?' asked Ali.

But Ben Josef would not tell him. 'I do not know,' he answered; 'I only know that it will certainly come.'

Chapter VII

♦

The Adventure of the Dragon's Teeth

Henceforward Ali and the White Camel joined Sheikh Heber and travelled over the desert with the camp. They loved this life better than the peace of the oasis, and when presently Heber and his men and horses and camels returned to the Purple Mountains, they found all well and were welcomed gladly. Heart's Delight rejoiced to see her husband and her son again, and on hearing of the things that had been done she approved of them and felt sure that Sheikh Khalid, who came of an ancient race, would never more think evil of Heber, or seek to do him a hurt.

'There is goodness hidden in every man's heart,' she said, 'and mercy is the surest key to reach it.'

When the grasses about the encampment were

eaten down and the herds cried for fresh food, the Bedouins moved onward, still travelling to the south, and at last they came to the limit of their domains and reached a ridge of low, porphyry hills called the Dragon's Teeth, because they were scattered along ten miles of the desert and sprouted out of the sandy waste. They were made of red granite, and amongst them stretched regions of good browse and opened some precious water-holes. For the Red Desert it was a fertile place, and Sheikh Heber had sometimes wondered if it might be handled skillfully and even planted with date-palms and turned into an oasis. But the water-supply was uncertain and his husbandmen advised him not to attempt it. The land lay upon Heber's boundaries and beyond it extended the kingdom of Sheikh Khalid.

And now a dreadful thing happened, for Heart's Delight fell sick and grew pale and thin and could not eat her food. This made the camp very sad, and Sheikh Heber and Ali kept close to her and comforted her and did all in their power to cure her. They were now more than two hundred miles from home and Heart's Delight was not strong enough to make such a journey at present. They tried everything, and the doctor of the camp, who was a clever old Arab and skilled at most of the ailments his people suffered, could not cure the Sheikh's wife. Neither was Fatima, her own waiting-woman, able to do anything. She adored Heart's Delight and had served her faithfully ever since she was a child, and she would have given her life for her mistress if that were any use.

There came a day when Fatima spoke with Heart's

Delight and implored her to eat and drink a little; and Ali's mother, knowing how glad people often are to run about and do something when those they love are lying sick, said to Fatima:

'I think that I could eat a little scrap of jugged hare. So tell Ali to take his gun and set off at once and shoot one for me.'

Heart's Delight did not really want a jugged hare, or anything else, but she knew that her son was mooning about, idle and miserable, and thought it would occupy his mind to have some sport in the hills.

And the moment Ali heard this, he fetched his gun and ran to Ben Josef and made him kneel down and mounted quickly. Then he told Ben the good news, that Heart's Delight thought she could eat some jugged hare. Ali did not use a saddle now. He would just leap on to the white camel's back and away they would go.

Ben set off swiftly, and soon they reached the hills, where sport was always to be found. Indeed, the boy had already shot quail and partridge and a mountain goat for his mother; but none of these things tempted her, though they were made as delicious as the camp cook could make them.

Now Ben Josef knelt down and sat patiently while Ali, gun in hand, crept over the scrub and looked out for a hare. Before very long the lad spotted a big one feeding. He was a clever and cunning hare and knew a gun when he saw one, for people had shot at him before and fortunately missed. Now the difficulty was that Ali knew the way in which wild things think and could see life with their eyes and understand their language; and, of course, it is very hard to kill any-body who begins to talk and wants to argue with you.

But just as he aimed and was going to shoot, the hare sat up and lifted his front paws and cried:

'Comrade!'

Ali hardened his heart, however, and was just going to pull the trigger and shoot, whether the hare was a comrade or no, when the creature begged for a word or two. So Ali beckoned, to see if it would come, and the wily hare came – rather slowly – for he was thinking hard all the time how to get out of this mess.

'My camel, Ben Josef, will better understand you than I can,' said Ali, 'so follow me, please, and listen to the good reason why it is certain that I must shoot you.'

'Nothing is certain until it has happened, noble young man,' answered the hare. Then he followed Ali to where Ben Josef sat nibbling his favourite spurges.

Then Ali and the hare squatted down beside him and the hare learned the reason for his sad fate.

'My dear mother, the wife of Sheikh Heber, is very sick and can eat nothing,' began Ali. 'But today she has felt that a little jugged hare would do her all the good in the world, and she has a great fancy for it. I am her son and have come to the hills to get her a hare and have found you.'

'I see – I quite see,' answered the hare. 'You mustn't think me fussy; but I have a queer feeling that I should hate to be jugged. Not that I should let my own feelings stand between me and your dear mother, but there are several reasons against such a plan.'

'What do you mean by "fussy"?' asked Ali. 'What is fussiness exactly?'

'To be fussy is always wanting things just your own way, without caring if it is anybody else's way,' explained the hare. 'Fussiness is to give pleasure to yourself, and not mind in the least if you are being a nuisance to other people. But I am not like that, noble young man. My simple rule is the greatest happiness for the greatest number, and if I thought that I should really improve your mother's health by dying for her, I should say, "Shoot me and jug me at once!"

'She must be a grand woman to have such a son as you are,' he continued.

Then Ben Josef spoke.

'Do not flatter, hare,' he said. 'Ali has no use for flattery.'

'You will be doing a splendid deed,' declared Ali 'You will have the joy of knowing that your life has ended in a useful manner and that you may have preserved the life of somebody far more important than yourself. You will be remembered honourably and thought upon kindly.'

'There are no doubt many more important lives than mine,' replied the hare. 'Nobody knows that better than I do; but it is wonderful how important one's own life seems to be at a moment like this, when a terrible gun is at one's elbow and the future looks so exceedingly black. Still,' he continued, 'you are perfectly right, as a great sheikh's son naturally would be; but for one unfortunate fact, I should not beg to live another moment. It is this: I am very, very old. I am tough and stringy and lean and long past my prime. In a word, I should make an utterly wretched jugged hare – not at all the sort of dish for your magnificent, but sick, mother. In fact I feel perfectly certain that I should make her worse. Why, I might even finish her off altogether!'

'You are lying, hare,' said Ben Josef sternly. 'You are in splendid condition – in your prime and as fat as butter. I never saw a hare more perfectly suited to being jugged.'

'I am sorry you lied,' said Ali. 'I would rather you had gone game.'

'A hare always goes game,' answered the other, 'because he is game. But one more thought occurs to me. Granted, for the sake of argument, that I should jug as well as anybody else – though it isn't true – yet consider if your gracious and blessed mother is right in wanting jugged hare at all. To be jugged for her is utterly splendid – I quite see that now – I want to be. I long to be. But invalids often beg for things that are by no means good for them, and if she is as ill as you say, then I cannot help feeling that a rich, spicy dish like jugged hare might be very bad indeed for her.'

Ali turned to Ben Josef.

'Shall I shoot him and have done with him?' he asked; and while Ben considered, the hare made a final suggestion and played his trump card as they say.

'Just turn your gun into the air for a minute longer,' he said, 'because by good luck I can be more useful to you alive than jugged after all. If I tell you something that may be of the greatest importance to your dear mother, will you let me off?'

'Certainly I will,' answered Ali. 'But you know perfectly well you can't.'

'Listen to him,' directed Ben Josef. 'I shall see if he tells another story.'

'It is like this,' explained the hare. 'Within ten

miles of the Dragon's Teeth, due east, lies the encampment of great Sheikh Khalid. He is there with his people on good ground grazing his flocks. I go there myself of a night sometimes for a bite of their excellent grass, and I happen to know that in the camp Khalid has a magnificent doctor – one of the wisest of all the Bedouin doctors. His name is Sage Tarik and he is famous all over the Red Desert. If by chance, therefore, you are friends with Sheikh Khalid, you cannot do better than go to see him at once and borrow Sage Tarik for your blessed mother.'

Ali looked at the White Camel and Ben Josef wasted not a word. 'The hare has spoken truth for once, and we will do this thing and hasten to Khalid,' he said. 'Jump up, Ali.'

'One more word,' added their new friend as they prepared to depart. 'If Sage Tarik should say that jugged hare is needful to cure the suffering lady, then I am ready and willing to do my part. I promise faithfully to meet you here in exactly a week and put myself in your hands. I can't say more than that.'

'You can't,' admitted Ali, 'and I will come in exactly a week and tell you how things are. What is your name, by the way?'

'Rupert,' said the hare.

'There is no such name,' answered Ali, 'and you know it.'

'It is not an Arabian name, I grant you,' replied Rupert, 'but it is a real name for all that. Hiding behind a stone I once listened to some explorers – men with white faces and one called another "Rupert", and I thought it such a fine name that I have called myself Rupert ever since.'

'Come,' cried Ben Josef; 'we waste time.'

And a moment later he and Ali sped away due east over the desert to the encampment of Sheikh Khalid.

The sun had set by the time they reached their old enemy's tents; but it was still light, and a rare and lovely mauve and rose afterglow trembled above the encampment as Ben, who had come at a tremendous pace and done the ten miles in less than an hour, strode among the tents. And many men, who remembered the battle and the dreadful things he did against them, were terrified to see the White Camel again and feared that his coming might mean trouble. But he stopped in the midst of them, and Ali dismounted and spoke to the strange Arabs kindly and asked them to tell Sheikh Khalid that he was come into the camp and begged to be allowed to see him.

Some time had passed since the day when Khalid returned to his people; but he remembered Ali and Ben Josef well enough and now he himself came to the visitors. With him also walked a boy and a girl. They were his son and daughter, and the lad was called Salem and his sister was called Morning Star. They were a beautiful pair, and Morning Star amazed Ali with her loveliness, for he had never seen such a girl in his life, and didn't know there was such a girl in the world.

Khalid welcomed them kindly, and his dark face lit up with joy and his eyes flashed to see Ali and Ben Josef.

'This is a good and pleasant thing to happen, Ali,' he said, 'and I hope that all is well with your parents and yourself. And if you come to ask me a favour, or demand from me any service that I can do for Sheikh Heber, I shall make haste to do it.'

Then the Sheikh turned to his children and introduced them to Ali, and they made friends at once and were glad to meet one of whom their father had often spoken with great praise.

And while Ali heard Morning Star's voice and thought it sweeter than the chiming of camel bells, she listened to him and looked into his eyes and felt that he was a very charming young man and well worth knowing. Ali told his tale, and while Sheikh Khalid mourned to know that Heart's Delight was so ill, he rejoiced to have the chance to be useful to her. He called for Sage Tariki, and an old but genial doctor, with a perfect bedside manner, listened to Ali's story. The boy could not tell him much, and he said that it would be necessary for him to see the patient and study her case before he could attempt to do her good, so Khalid ordered an immediate start, and when Ali and Ben Josef had both enjoyed a splendid meal, four camels set forth for the camp of Heber under the Dragon's Teeth.

Ben led the way with Ali, and Sheikh Khalid came next on a big dromedary, while Sage Tarik followed, and the fourth camel carried all the medicines for Heart's Delight, because the doctor was leaving nothing to chance and did not want to find, when he reached his patient, that he had left at home just the physic he most needed.

Ali told Sheikh Khalid about the hare, and the chief guessed that Rupert must have been sent by Allah. Indeed, he became very hopeful for Heber's wife when he heard the story, and felt that Tarik was pretty sure to make her well.

They padded along through the moonlight and at

last arrived, and while Ali called Fatima from his mother's tent and she told Tarik all about the case, Sheikh Heber in much amazement learned that Ali had returned to camp with Sheikh Khalid. So he hastened out to see him, and the two sheikhs embraced with friendship and were glad to meet again.

Heber ordered a banquet to be spread for Khalid, and they ate and drank together and waited to hear of what Sage Tarik thought of Ali's mother. But he did not come for a long time, because after he had seen Heart's Delight and studied her case with all his great learning and experience, he went to his medicines and worked away for a long while among them and presently produced one small pill and gave it to the patient himself.

Then, directing Fatima what to do and promising to see Heart's Delight in the morning, Tarik joined his chief and Heber and told them all about the illness. But he was very hopeful indeed, and declared that the sick lady would certainly recover if she proved ready and willing to follow his advice.

'I shall abide in your camp, Sheikh Heber, for several days,' said Tarik, 'and, if all goes well, by that time your wife will take a turn for the better. There is nothing dangerous the matter with her and I believe that she will soon be strong again, because she is still young and Nature always takes the side of youth.'

Next morning Sheikh Khalid returned to his people, and Heber said comfortable words and thanked him and declared it was a great compliment that his friend should have come himself. And Khalid promised to return again in a few days, and hoped that he might see Heart's Delight when he did so. And Ali begged the Sheikh to bring his son and daughter with him, so that his parents might see them.

'My mother would dearly love Morning Star,' said Ali, and Sheikh Khalid smiled in his heart, because when young men say that their mothers would love young maidens, then it is possible they may be loving them themselves.

So the Sheikh went on his way, but the doctor stopped with Heber and soon did wonders for Heart's Delight. Sage Tarik was indeed a very great man and deeply skilled in the art of healing. The camp grew more and more cheerful to hear such good news, and many of the people saw their chieftain's wife and were welcomed and able to tell the rest that Heart's Delight was getting better and better and making a splendid and complete recovery. And presently she came out from her tent and sat among her nearest and dearest friends, and all men praised Tarik for the grand thing he had done with his cleverness and his physics.

Ali never forgot a promise, and when a week was past he remembered that he was to meet Rupert, the hare. Therefore he asked Sage Tarik if jugged hare would be good for his mother.

'No,' answered Tarik. 'Not at all. Quite out of the question. It will still be a long time before Sheikh Heber's wife can safely partake of jugged hare.'

And Ali was glad, because he knew that Rupert would be thankful, so he set off to tell him. On the back of Ben Josef he went; but he did not take his gun.

'If he does not see the gun,' he said, 'Rupert will feel more at peace.'

As a matter of fact, however, Rupert saw nothing. I am sorry to say that he had not kept his word and was miles and miles away from his old haunts when Ali arrived with the good news.

Rupert, you see, had thought it over and he had decided that the risks were too great. 'If I knew Sage Tarik would not allow this woman to eat jugged hare, then all would be well,' he said to himself, 'but what happens exactly if Tarik prescribes jugged hare and says that is just what she wants to cure her? "Safety first" is a very good motto after all.' So, little guessing that Ali was coming to thank him and bring him a fat lettuce and a ball of bran and a bunch of grapes – all things he adored – Rupert felt there was nothing like safety first, and made a bolt for it while the going was good.

When Ali arrived, Rupert was twenty miles away, and though the young man called him many times and assured him that he was safe, of course no answer came. So he turned to Ben Josef and said,

'I'm very much afraid Rupert has told us another lie; but he doesn't really matter, does he?'

And Ben answered,

'Not a bit. When you come down to bed-rock, nobody really matters.'

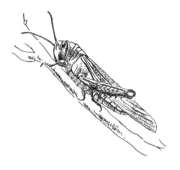

Chapter VIII

♦

The Adventure of the Locusts

When he returned to his camp, Sheikh Khalid sent a messenger far north to fertile lands and presently dispatched to Heart's Delight a gift of golden dates and purple figs. He sent rice also and choice cakes, sweetmeats, and everything that a sick person could possibly like. But though Ali's mother now began to get well very fast and feel hungry again, after he had told her the story of Rupert, she never asked for jugged hare, but said that was the one thing she didn't fancy in the least. Then she grew strong and happy, so Sage Tarik packed up his medicines and prepared to go back to his master. Heart's Delight blessed him for making her well again and gave him a jewel of great beauty.

CHAPTER VIII

It was a topaz as large as a tangerine orange and as glowing and full of delicious light as the risen sun.

Tarik took it and said that it would be a joy to his wife and an heirloom in his family for ever more. So he departed, and Sheikh Heber and Ali went with him, to say goodbye to Khalid and thank him for his great goodness. And they carried gifts for him and Salem, his son, and Morning Star, his daughter. Heber gave Sheikh Khalid a grand young Arab charger and a magnificent sword of Damascus steel with a hilt of ivory and silver. And Ali brought Salem a pair of pistols, rich in fine workmanship; but for Morning Star he had won another jewel from his mother, for Heart's Delight, strange to say, didn't care twopence for jewellery, and she had given Ali a wondrous necklace of pink pearls for Sheikh Khalid's daughter.

The invalid was now well enough to travel, and in a few days Heber's people set their faces to the north and began the long journey homeward. But one rather interesting thing happened at the encampment of Khalid, for Ben Josef had fallen in love with a beautiful young dromedary of the highest class, and she had fallen in love with him. She was called Light of Day and the white camel asked Ali if he might have her for his wife, and Ali asked Sheikh Khalid, and the Sheikh said that Ben was welcome to her. So now Ben Josef became a married camel, though it did not make him take himself any more seriously, because to take himself seriously was the one thing Ben could never do.

As they journeyed homeward by easy stages, Seyf made little expeditions on his own account, for he was a restless dwarf and liked to wander off by himself sometimes. He was gone three days with his camel on one of these lonely jaunts, and he came back rather thankfully and said that he had seen one of the most awful spots in the whole Red Desert.

'It is a fearful place,' he told them, 'and I hope I may never see it again. A low, long cliff as black as ink, rises out of the sand and about it lies a region of black stone, pitiless and evil. Nothing with life homes there. You shall not see a blade of grass, or a sprig of camel-thorn, or a leaf of any herb. Not even the cactus can live in that horrible earth. Not a jerboa hops there, not even a jackal comes within a mile of it, nor shall you hear the note of any bird, or see so much as a vulture in the sky above you. All is death and desolation, and above this valley of black ashes the black cliff scowls, so that you feel he is hating you and would destroy you if he could.'

'I think that I know where you have been,' said Sheik Heber, 'and it is indeed the most dreadful place in all my desert.'

He then unrolled his map and presently showed them the spot that Seyf had visited.

'It is the Cliff of the Simoom,' he told them, 'and many people say that a demon dwells there; but he is one of Nature's demons with nothing contrary to Nature about him. The black cliff is the haunt of Simoom – the poison wind which takes toll of the lives of men and beasts and is the most fearful thing you can face in the desert. For some reason it harbours at the black cliffs and will often leap out from them upon a traveller and keep baleful eyes always open to destroy the solitary wanderer, or the caravan.

You were fortunate to escape from it, dwarf, for had it wakened and leapt upon you and your camel, you must both have perished.'

'Simoom shall not have another chance,' promised Seyf, and Sheikh Heber warned Ali against the evil spot, little guessing that in time to come his son and the White Camel would be called to go there on a tremendous adventure and face the mysteries and horrors of that gloomy place. So they travelled homeward, and Ben's wife, Light of Day, had the pleasure of carrying Sheikh Heber's wife. Sometimes, for she loved camel-riding better than being carried in a palanquin.

Then happened a thing to make all the company very anxious. Of late many locusts had been seen going northward, and now their flights began to grow larger, until not seldom the sky was actually darkened by millions of the creatures on the wing together. They drew a pallid gauze against the blue of the sky and the glory of the sun, and would pass through the air like a cloud, only to give place to another huge flight an hour later. Sheikh Heber and his people knew the meaning of the locusts only too well, and hoped that they might wing on their terrible errand far away from the oasis. Once, many years before, the pest had fallen upon it and brought great sorrow and death, for man is powerless to conquer locust when he comes by the myriad. Then he devours every growing crop and opening leaf, until happy lands are turned into a wilderness and the dwellers therein see their cattle starve and their little children cry for food.

But Heber pushed on, hoping for the best, yet greatly fearing because the flights of the locusts increased; and where they encamped from time to time it was only to find the insects before them. They stood face to face with a great plague, therefore, and the spirits of the Bedouin people sank and the camp was full of anxious faces and troubled eyes. For still locusts veiled the midday sun aloft and the hiss of their innumerable wings sounded faintly upon the ear of those beneath.

The Arabs cooked and ate thousands of locusts for a time, because they were quite wholesome and made a change; but nobody enjoyed them very much, thinking only of the great peril they promised and the danger they threatened to all things that live by grass and herb. They were prepared for the worst, therefore, yet hoped for the best and travelled steadily forward with stock that already began to grow a little hungry as the browse upon their scattered feeding-grounds grew thinner. And then they came to the oasis and knew the worst, for the locusts had come before them, done terrible evil and spread waste and desolation everywhere.

The old folk who never left it told how in one night vast swarms of the insects had settled upon the oasis until grass and corn and every green tree crawled with them; and Sheikh Heber gazed upon his domain and counted the cost and knew that long, lean years would have to pass by before any recovery could be hoped for.

For the present there was nothing to do but fight the locusts day and night and put everybody on rations. The people of course understood and knew they might have to go short for many a long day, but the poor animals could not understand at all, though

Chapter VIII

Ben Josef tried to make the camels learn what had happened. Time passed and the clan grew thin and their beasts very poor. The locusts indeed were gone at last, but they left a very sad state of affairs behind them, and Sheikh Heber drew out his map again and considered his country and where best to take his flocks, for browse around the oasis was terribly scanty now and would need much time before it grew green and rich again.

He decided to divide the clan and take part to one place and part to another, and he hoped to find some grazing-grounds at no very great distance away, where the locusts had not fallen and where herbage might be found for his hungry creatures. There was one such spot about sixty or seventy miles distant from the oasis; but before he dispatched a company to this region, Heber bade Ali mount Ben Josef and ride there and find out if the place could promise food and whether a wadi that ran through the midst of it contained good water. So Ali set off on Ben Josef, who poor fellow, was grown rather thin now, for he ate as little as he possibly could and, when he came upon a good bite of grass now and then in some shel- tered nook, always made Light of Day eat it. She wanted to share his finds with him, but he made her eat them all.

Seyf, the dwarf, went with Ali upon this journey, and the three friends talked together and hoped that luck would soon turn and things get better for the clan.

'What we want is money,' said Seyf. 'Money would buy everything, and if we had money, we could carry it to the cities of Arabia the Blessed, and, in exchange for it, we should get huge loads of fodder for the cattle, and meal and grain and oil and a thousand other things for ourselves.'

'As we have no gold to mention, we must fall back on goodness,' said Ali, 'and save ourselves by our own pluck and courage.'

'Goodness is a poor substitute for gold in a mess like this,' replied Seyf. 'Goodness butters no man's bread. It is gold that counts in the world of men. There are, of course, far more good people than rich people; but if you want comfort and applause and attention on bended knees and a fat tummy, then the easiest way to get them is to be rich. Gold is said to be the root of all evil, but I never met anybody who was not quite ready to nibble that root if he got a chance.'

'I did not know until now how important a thing it may be to have money,' answered Ali 'One has never felt the need of it before; but my father's chest is nearly empty now and he may have to sell my mother's pretty, precious stones very soon.'

'She will not mind in the least,' said the White Camel. 'Jewels are of no account to Heart's Delight.'

'It is a very horrible thought all the same that they should have to go,' declared Ali, but Ben, who was in rather a wise sort of mood, contradicted him.

'Not horrible,' he explained. 'It is a thing that may happen owing to the locusts. Nature works in this way. There is a cause for a thing and then there is the effect that follows. And if you have a certain cause, like the locusts, then you get a certain effect, like starvation for those deprived of their food. But there is nothing horrible about it. It would be very horrible indeed if there were a cause and no effect from it, because that were contrary to Nature.'

But neither Ali nor Seyf was feeling wise, so they told Ben Josef to shut up and not try to be too clever.

In two marches they reached the grazing-ground, and their eyes were made glad, for green grass rewarded them and amid the rocks of the wadi there were good signs of water. Seyf knew the place and hastened to the best well that all might drink their fill; but somebody was already at the well, and they stood still and stared at a huge snake lying curled up in a circle round the well-head. It was a magnificent but formidable monster about as long as a cricket pitch, and on its brown, bright skin shone a beautiful pattern of silver and orange spots with streaks of emerald green and peacock blue.

'Shoot it before it wakes up, and be quick about it,' cried Seyf.

But Ali hesitated.

'It may not be a poisonous snake,' he said.

'The only good snake is a dead snake,' answered Seyf. 'Don't argue about it. Such a serpent as this should be slain at sight.'

But Ben Josef spoke. He knew that, with their gift of language, it would be possible to talk to the snake.

'He is perfectly harmless and very old,' said Ben. 'We can at least try to make him a friend, and if he refuses to be a friend, then we will learn why.'

The snake had awakened at their voices. He lifted his head and his wonderful eyes shone like diamonds upon them. He was going to make a bolt for it; but Ben Josef called to him and he understood and turned round and crept a little nearer.

'Let us be friends, snake,' said Ali. 'You may be able to tell us things that we want to know. This is my father's grazing-land and we should like to hear if you have had many locusts.'

'They came, but stayed not long,' replied the snake. 'I ate them until I was tired of them – several million I should think. They then departed and the grass has begun to grow again as you see.'

'Very good news,' declared Ali. 'Do you live here?'

'I have lived here before you were born and shall hope to go on living here for many years after you are dead,' replied the great snake.

'Be civil!' ordered Ben Josef. 'What has my master done to get such an answer as that?'

'He is a man,' answered the serpent, 'and men hate me and I hate all men but one. You are abominably unjust and cruel to my people and utterly fail to understand us.'

'That's what rascals always say when they are understood only too well,' replied Seyf. 'You are a sneaking, poisonous lot of scoundrels and nobody has any use for you and nobody knows why on earth Allah made you.'

'You speak like the ignorant little idiot you are,' replied the snake. 'We are not all poisonous and when we are, then our poison is our protection. You tar us all with the same brush and kill us without good cause; and you are too blind to see that a serpent such as myself, for example, is among the loveliest creatures that Allah ever made. There is no grace like our grace; there are no eyes like ours; no colours as beautiful as our colours.'

'Lucky you're so pleased with yourself,' said Seyf, 'for nobody else is.'

'What is your name?' asked Ali.

'I am called Abdullah,' answered the great snake. 'I am a hundred years old and among the noblest serpents that have ever lived. I have never seen such another in all my life, and no more has anybody else.'

'Are you married?' enquired Ben Josef.

'I am a bachelor,' replied Abdullah. 'I thought to marry half a century ago; but happily she wouldn't take me.'

'Why do you say 'happily'?' asked Ben.

'Because of what her husband told me afterwards,' answered Abdullah. 'She wedded somebody else and shortened his life by many years. But when he died, she married again, and this time her husband shortened her life by many years. In fact he killed her almost immediately.'

'That was justice,' suggested Ali.

'Yes – what they call poetic justice,' agreed the snake.

'And now,' continued Ali, 'tell us what you are good for, please.'

But Abdullah was furious at this question.

'Who's being rude now?' he asked. 'Nothing can be more impertinent than to ask a person what they are good for. And I retort with a tu quoque and ask you what you are good for.'

'What is a tu quoque?' asked Ali eagerly. 'That's something new to me.'

'Never mind – just tell me what you are good for yourself?' hissed Abdullah.

Ali felt abashed.

'Well, of course, if you put it so, I'm certainly not good for very much,' he admitted.

'I thought not!' said the snake triumphantly; and then Seyf spoke up for Ali.

'Ali is the great Sheikh Heber's son, and will be a sheikh himself some day,' he said.

'Then the great Sheikh Heber should have taught him manners,' answered Abdullah. 'Noblesse oblige is a very sound saying.'

'He might have shot you when you were asleep,' continued the dwarf, 'but he was merciful and let you live.'

'Because you were so lovely,' said Ali.

'In that case I withdraw my hard words,' answered Abdullah. 'I never thought to be on terms of friendship with another human being; but at my age I would sooner make friends than enemies. I ask from Nature little more than sufficient to eat and freedom to go my own way always and do exactly what I like, when I like and how I like. That's reasonable enough, surely?'

'What do you eat?' asked Ali.

'Jackals, if I can catch them asleep,' replied Abdullah. 'In fact anything and everything. My bonne bouche is a hare.'

'Did you ever meet a hare called Rupert?' asked Ali.

'I couldn't tell you,' replied Abdullah. 'That's a curious name for a hare.'

'He was a curious hare,' said Ali. Then he spoke again.

'There seems to be plenty of good grass, but we must travel the whole grazing-grounds and see if the locusts have spared enough for us.'

Now, Ben Josef, who had been listening quietly to Abdullah, asked him a question.

'You speak very well, Abdullah,' he said, 'and seem to know foreign languages too, but you didn't learn all those fine words in the desert, so where did you learn them?'

'I learned them in the desert,' replied the great snake, 'because I have never been off the desert; but you will remember that when I said I hated men, I added "all but one man." There is a man who sometimes comes here to gather herbs which grow in the wadi. He is old and wise, and being wise he knows that we serpents are also very wise – in fact the wisest things in the world. And it is our wisdom, no doubt, which makes us dislike and distrust men so much. We have seen what happens to the birds and beasts that trust you.'

'Who is this wise man and where does he live?' asked Ali.

'I do not know where he may live,' replied Abdullah, 'but it cannot be very far off because he is old and travels slowly.'

'The wisest man in the world,' said Ali, 'is Sage Tarik, who made my mother well again when she was ill.'

'No, my friend is far wiser than anybody,' declared Abdullah. 'He is wise enough to speak my language, and to him even we snakes are but children in wisdom. I doubt, if you met him, whether he would waste a moment of his time in talking to you.'

'Then he would not be wise,' said Ben Josef, 'because everybody may be worth talking to.'

'He is called Jameel,' explained Abdullah; 'just that and no more. He does not like to be called a sage and does not claim to be a teacher; but he cannot help teaching, because he knows such a number of interesting things. It needs to be a pretty clever person to tell me anything I don't know already, but he can.'

'I hope that we shall meet him,' said Ali.

'I hope you may,' replied Abdullah, 'and I hope you will have the wits to understand him if you do.'

They left the vain old snake soon afterwards, and, before they parted, he was fairly amiable

'I have now two men friends,' he said. 'You can never be such a friend as Jameel, but you were clever enough to see how amazingly beautiful I am and decent enough not to shoot me. So you may consider that I am one of your supporters in future. And should you bring your flocks to this region, I will help you to look after them. But warn your people to do me no hurt if they see me.'

Ali told him about the oasis and Abdullah said that he would look in some day when he had nothing better to do.

They travelled on for five miles and were glad to mark a plain of fairly good grass extending through the desert sands. And Seyf, who was skilled in all such matters, said that the sheep would do better here for a time than at the oasis; so they went home with the news.

Sheikh Heber was glad, and before long he sent the greater number of his sheep to this pasture with trusty men to tend them.

But the times were very bad; Heber's money had all gone in buying food, and precious beasts began to grow too thin to live. Then many good camels died of hunger and the little children lacked for milk because even the milking camels had to suffer. And mothers wept and fathers cried against Allah, and things began to look very bad indeed.

Then there came a day when Sheikh Heber called Ali to him and spoke of the past.

'When I was young,' he said, 'and your grand-father, Sheikh Abbas, reigned over the clan, we were once faced with great trouble, even as we are now. And my father bade me mount my steed and take a companion and seek out a hermit – a famous dreamer – who lived in the desert. We were to tell him of our woe and beg him to let us hear if anything could be done about it. I obeyed at once, set off and visited the hermit.'

Heber brought out his map.

'Here you see this cross marked upon the parch-ment,' he said. 'That is where the wonderful man lives – perhaps no more than fifty miles from the spot where we have sent our sheep. I cannot now call to mind what he directed Sheikh Abbas to do; but I remember that he gave me a letter for my father, for among other great gifts he could write. And I also remember that Sheikh Abbas did what this rare prophet told him to do. From that day things began to get better with us, and in one year from that time all was well.'

'Does he still live – this splendid dreamer?' asked Ali.

'Everything of course turns upon that,' replied his father. 'If, as may be most likely, he has passed away, then your journey will be in vain; but if he still lives, then, such are his great gifts that he may know how to save us. And if he will listen to you and send me some advice, I shall take it and do exactly as he may tell me.'

'What is his name?' asked Ali.

'He is called Jameel,' replied Sheikh Heber; and then Ali remembered the past and what Abdullah had told him. He had let his parents hear all about the snake, and they were not surprised, because they knew Ali had the gift to talk to wild creatures; but the boy had quite forgotten about Jameel until his father reminded him.

'I can say one good thing to start with, my father,' he answered, 'and that one good thing may lead to better things. Jameel lives! Abdullah, the serpent, knows him well and says that he is the wisest of all men.'

'Good!' answered Heber. 'And if he is wise enough to feed starving children and put flesh on my poor beasts and cattle, then I will agree with your big snake and say no man is wiser than Jameel. Start upon Ben Josef tomorrow; visit the shepherds on your way and then seek out Jameel and tell him our sad story, my son.'

So Ali set off at moon-rise that very night upon the White Camel, and Ben Josef was hopeful from the first and believed that good would come of it.

'It will be splendid for you to see and hear this hermit,' he said, 'and he will surely be kind to me also, because real wisdom is never lacking in friendship for all created things. To be alive at all is to earn the right of kindness and goodwill from your fellow mortals; and Jameel will be sure to know that.'

Chapter IX

◆

The Adventure of the Dreamer

Ben Josef made one of his grand forced marches and strode over the desert with rare speed, for time was precious. He did not talk much and his thoughts were rather sad, because he had just lost his mother, Morgiana. She had not died from want, for the famine was not allowed to lessen her portion of food; but she had reached to thirty years, which is a camel's span of life, and so she passed peacefully away. And Ben missed her a good deal, though Light of Day did the best she could to comfort him.

He and Ali were now seventeen years old and in splendid health; but, like everybody else, they went short of food and were always rather hungry. They made nothing of it all the same, and Ben Josef had never sped better than on the journey to the hermit. In one day he did the two days' work, and when night came again Ali and he had reached the ground where Heber's flock-masters watched over his sheep. And they rested there and slept that night.

Another good march brought them to the strange home of Jameel, and they came upon a little ring of rose-red granite hills, where, sunk amidst them, lay the tiniest oasis in the whole desert. Three date-palms stood there and a patch of cultivated land, and a twinkle of green grass shone in the lap of the little hills, while under the palms stood a small house made of the granite and looking like a pink pearl set in emeralds.

Here all alone dwelt old Jameel without any protection whatever. But he was his own protection because the wandering Arabs knew him well, and for two generations of the people he had ever befriended them and helped them when it was in his power to do so. His goodness had made him safe from all men, and since he knew the language of every desert creature, he was safe from them also.

The three palm-trees gave him nearly all the food he wanted, and for the rest he had his patch of Guinea corn and an orange-tree and a little well of pure water.

Now Jameel stood at the door of his house to welcome Ali and Ben Josef. They saw an immensely tall, smiling old fellow with a brown, wrinkled face and gentle eyes. There was not a hair on Jameel's head, and it shone like old polished ivory in the sun. He wore an outer coat of camel's hair and beneath it a linen robe of dazzling whiteness.

'Hail, little brother!' he said, 'and hail, White Camel. Leap off his back, Ali, then you shall both eat the meal that I have prepared for you.'

Amazed that Jameel had expected them, Ali soon fell to upon some fine dates and crisp cakes, while Ben found a heap of his favourite spurge awaiting him, fresh cut, rich and full of sap.

When they had eaten and rested well and the sun was sunk into the desert they all sat together and watched the stars come out, and Jameel spoke to them in the language that both could understand.

'Tomorrow,' he said, 'you shall tell me all you have to tell. Tonight we will chat together and I shall have the pleasure of hearing your young voices in my ears.'

'We have come to listen and learn, not to talk, great Jameel,' said Ali.

'I am not at all great except in body,' replied the hermit. 'Nature has made me seven feet tall – a giant – but after that feat, she was tired and forgot all about my wits. I do not know enough to teach anybody, Ali, but I am always learning still and welcome knowledge. Everything and everybody can teach you something, yet all that I know so far is like this pinch of sand between my finger and thumb compared to the desert. It were easier to count the sand grains in the three Arabias than to master one's fill of knowledge. But how much more we might know if we took the trouble to learn! Heart and head are both needful to wisdom, and knowledge without wisdom is a date without its stone.'

'How comes it there are schoolmasters if nobody knows enough to teach, dear Jameel?' asked Ali.

'I cannot tell you,' answered the ancient. 'But a

good school-master must try to learn his pupil first before he would teach him, for learning depends more upon the learner than the teacher, and there are many things that some boys and girls can never learn, because the gift of learning them is not there. To think is the great thing, and according to your power of thinking, so will the power of learning be. A schoolmaster should learn how much gift for thinking the pupil may have. Then he will find what ground lies before him whereon to sow the seed of knowledge. Thus he will learn what to sow and what not to sow, and what crop is most likely to spring up and bear good fruit. But schoolmasters cannot do these fine things. Children are taught in gangs, and their power to think taken for granted rather than proved.'

'It seems very hard to know anything at all for certain,' said Ali.

'Very hard indeed,' agreed Jameel. 'If a man can say he knows – say ten things – for certain, then he may be called a clever fellow. But he must know them for certain and be able to tell other people why they are true. New knowledge flows about us like the light of the sun, and the new knowledge is ever trying to drown the old knowledge. But you must remember that youth and age have nothing to do with truth. Though it is old, a thing may still be quite true; and though it is new, it may yet be false.'

'Is a thing true in one place and false in another?' asked Ali.

'No,' replied Jameel. 'If it is true in one place, it is true everywhere. People's ideas about things, such as how to behave, for example, are very different, but truth lies outside our ideas. Most people talk like parrots and just echo what they have read, or what has been dinned into their ears, without thinking about it; yet they cannot reach truth in that way. A certainty is very rare, and the search for it very difficult. But men will never cease trying to find truth, and the hunting is well worth our trouble even though we fail to find it. Every success of any importance is built on many failures to succeed, so when you fail to find truth, do not be cast down, but feel your failure is only one step nearer to your success. All wisdom is merely picking and choosing from what life spreads before us, and the very wisest man is sure to make mistakes and pick a good many wrong things.'

'Men are but young creatures to their dying day,' said Ben Josef. 'They do not grow up and become old as we other creatures do. They make so many more mistakes than we camels do, for instance.'

'Most true, Ben,' declared Jameel. 'The fact is that we men were all babies yesterday and have a long way to go before we grow up. Earth herself is only a fat, round baby compared with many of the stars shining above our heads tonight; and sometimes, in sad moments, I have been tempted to think that we men, who swarm over Earth's beautiful body, are only one of her childish complaints – a sort of nettle rash which will presently pass away and leave her the happier and cleaner without us. But that is only a horrid idea I get when I have eaten too many millet cakes and am feeling bad inside. It isn't true; and when I feel well, as I do now talking to you two young people, I would rather say that Mother Earth is an artist for ever busy in making beautiful things. And when she grows old and cannot make any more beautiful things, she will count over her works and weigh them, and perhaps decide that, after all, men and women and boys and girls were the very best things she ever made.'

'And perhaps camels,' ventured Ben Josef.

'And camels most certainly,' assented Jameel. 'You camels are the most wonderful people, Ben, and I have often envied your amazing powers to do without food and sleep.'

'Men are certainly very sleepy and very greedy sometimes,' said Ali, 'and often the greedier they are, the sleepier they are.'

'Human beings,' declared the White Camel, 'do not get half as much out of their lives as they might, seeing how well they are made to enjoy life. They have many more gifts than we four-footed and winged people, and yet a prosperous camel, like myself, really enjoys being alive much more than the most prosperous man ever does.'

'We have got so much more to think about and worry over than you,' explained Ali, 'and so much more to think with, for that matter.'

'Think by all means, but why worry so much?' asked Ben Josef. 'And if thinking only brings worry, then why think? Great Jameel says that children should be taught how to think; but what's the use of that, if thinking only stains their young faces with lines and spoils their beauty and doesn't bring any real happiness to their little hearts?'

'You are right and wrong both, Ben,' answered Jameel, 'and first I will tell you what you said that was right. Camels do get more out of life than most men and women, because they know how to be alive all over, with every bit of them – their splendid bodies and their modest brains. The grand thing is surely to be alive with every bit of us – not only a piece here and there. We should give the whole of us a chance: that is only fair. Brain and muscles, teeth and tongue, legs and arms and wits – not a day should pass and leave any of them idle. Use every blessed bit of yourself. Get the best out of every toe when you run, and every finger when you toil with your hands, and every twist and turn of your mind when it is your mind you are trying to use at work or play. Nature never forgets to do her share, and the better you do your share, the better she will do hers; so pour yourself out, and when part of your wonderful body is tired, then give it a rest and use another part. Never let them all be idle together. Be as busy for them when you are awake as Nature is busy for them when you are asleep. And never, never, never tell anybody you don't know what to do, because you might as well say at once that you are a silly little fool and not worth the bread-and-butter you eat to keep you going. In a word, use the whole of yourself for all you are worth, and as practice makes perfect, then in good time you will become really useful to those who matter a great deal more than you do yourself – as the camels are.'

'Hear! Hear!' said Ben Josef.

'And one more thing,' added the old man, 'since you are both so patient with me and such good listeners. Don't let life run you into a mould if you can help it. Life has a deadly art to run us into a mould and let us grow cold and solid. A hermit like myself knows that only too well. Don't, therefore, pride yourself on always being the same. Try to see how different you can be. Keep your eyes open for new things to see and your wits for new things to think about. If you have only one idea, you miss all the other fine ideas that life is sure to offer you. They say that a rolling stone gathers no moss; but who wants to get mossy? So make yourself live all the time, and roll forward in mind and body from morning till night, for then you will learn what it means to be alive, if you have anything worth calling a brain in your head. Don't be content with merely existing; don't look on at life and never take a hand; don't watch people working and never work yourself; don't watch people playing and never play yourself; and, above all, don't read what other people have thought and never think yourself. Nothing is a greater mistake than that. And now I have talked quite enough. Talking is generally as idle as to sow the sand, or lecture a fool; but you are bright young people and will not be too bored.'

'What if health is denied you and you are sick and cannot live this splendid life, dear Jameel?' asked Ali, and the old man made answer.

'We did not build the houses that we live in, but if Allah has given us a better house than that in which our neighbour dwells, our first business and our first joy would be to visit his house and leave it not until we had made it as good as our own. And much may well be found in his house that is better than anything in our own, for a wise, sick man is doing far more good in the world than a healthy idiot. He may also be having a far better time, because he is making far better use of it.'

Ben Josef considered what Jameel had spoken on the main question.

'We creatures should give and take as Nature does,' he said. 'Then we shall not be half dead but all alive. We should treat Nature as we treat any other neighbour, and to respect her is to keep as healthy as she will let us and not talk nonsense about her. She doesn't talk any nonsense about us. Be healthy if you can, and if you cannot, still try to be wise.'

'Now sleep – both of you,' directed Jameel, 'and in the morning you shall tell me what is amiss with the clan and I will help Sheikh Heber and his people if I have the power.'

Ben rested his great neck upon the dewy earth, heaved a mighty sigh and went to sleep instantly, while Jameel brought Ali into his little house and they too quickly slumbered. Round about the jackals yelped and the hyenas laughed; but they all knew the hermit for a friend and never intruded upon his home unless they were in trouble, or wanted a word of advice.

Next morning Ali found that old Jameel knew everything already.

'You must be very wise to know what has happened to us,' he said. 'How could you tell that we have been smitten by the locusts and are become hungry and thirsty and poor, or that my father has spent his money and may no longer prosper unless something is done for us?'

'I dream dreams,' answered the hermit. 'I learn much from dreaming, both when I am awake and asleep. Thus the past and the future are as pictures, and I look both back and forward from my place midway between them.'

'Did you dream that Ben Josef and I were coming to you yesterday?' asked the young man.

'Yes, I did,' replied Jameel. 'I knew that you were coming and would be hungry, so I made ready. Your father came to me long years ago from his father, and I helped him with the troubles of that time. And I knew of the locusts and what they would do to Sheikh Heber and that he would send you to me yesterday. And I also know what is going to happen next. To know things before they happen is to remember the things that have already happened. But now tremendous things are going to happen to you that never happened before, and I hope you will come safely out of them.'

'If I can serve my clan, I will face them with all the courage they may need,' said Ali.

'This is what you will have to do,' replied Jameel. 'You are going to see a tremendous performance of Nature, and if you come out from her alive, you must thank Ben Josef for it. I feel sure myself that your White Camel, who is in many ways nearer to Nature than you are, will have the cleverness to pull you through.

'Now,' continued the old man, 'you must know that time is nothing to Nature. Centuries and seconds are all alike to her. Our time at best is short; but she is eternal and therefore doesn't bother about time. That's how she comes to do such a lot of things that seem utterly mad to us. With her flash of lightning she will slay the date-palm that took her a hundred years to build and bring to perfection; with her frost she will destroy a grove of orange-trees or nutmegs that men have toiled for generations to make perfect.

In a single night she will lay waste the work of her labour and her love. Or, as you know, she will send her locusts to ruin a beautiful oasis and lay all bare. She performs these mysteries because she chooses to do so, and the fact that her earthquakes knock down our houses and kill us when they fall, or her tempests wreck our ships and drown us when they sink, does not vex or worry Nature in the least, because she is no more interested in you and me than she is in all her other inventions. Yet from her tremendous deeds we men may sometimes reap good as well as evil if we have the sense to do so. I could tell you of a great many of her deeds where Nature seemed to be giving us a helping hand. But you must set out now, and if we meet again, I will tell you other things about her when we do.'

'I should like to hear what she is going to be at now,' said Ali.

'You will soon both hear and feel and see,' answered Jameel. 'You will watch her tremendous work for yourself, and after the mighty deed is done, you should be quite bright enough to see how at Allah's will Nature has performed a feat for Sheikh Heber and his little family that ought soon to get them out of their sorrow.'

'We trust you, dear Jameel,' said Ali. 'And what is Nature going to do, please, and where is she going to do it?'

'She is going to do something agreeable to herself,' explained the hermit. 'She is going to destroy with her great hand in one awful moment what her great hand created more than a million years ago. Yet to her this is no more than the sandcastle that a baby builds on the seashore for the next tide to sweep away again. And she is going to do it at the Cliff of the Simoom – that strange and savage place where men dread to go and where beasts and birds never think of going. But you must journey there with Ben Josef, and you cannot start too soon.'

'Is it very far?' asked Ali.

'But half a day's march with your faces to the south,' replied Jameel. 'I have store of provender for you both.'

'And after all is over, if it should still be well with us?' inquired Ben Josef.

'Then return as swiftly as you may to Sheikh Heber and tell him what has happened,' replied Jameel.

So they set off to the south; but not before Ali had thanked the old dreamer for his kindness and promised to visit him again if he should get the chance.

They talked about Jameel as they jogged along and agreed that he was a wonderful sort of man.

'He's very fond of hearing his own voice, apparently,' said Ben Josef; but Ali explained that.

'He gets so few chances,' he said.

As they came suddenly round a bluff of rock, an ostrich leapt up before them – a magnificent bird in full plumage with grand feathers that flashed in the sunlight all ebony and silver. He was rushing away at tremendous speed, but Ben Josef cried out to him that they were friends, and he understood and stopped.

'If you are friends,' he said, 'take care where you are walking. My wife's eggs are almost under your feet and our chicks should be hatched out tomorrow with any luck.'

Ben avoided the eggs and Ali hoped that the ostrich would have a good family.

'Probably not,' said the ostrich. 'Children are very disappointing as a rule and seldom give their parents half the kindness and affection that they get from them. They take us for granted rather too much in my opinion. But I may be wrong. I am not a very lucky bird and have got into a way of looking at the dark side of things rather too much perhaps.'

'How do you live in this desert?' asked Ali.

'I often wonder myself,' replied the ostrich. 'I pick up a living somehow.'

'It must be a jolly good living too,' said Ben Josef. 'I never saw an ostrich so plump and prosperous. Evidently you do yourself all right.'

'What is your name?' inquired Ali.

'I am called Mohammed, after the famous prophet,' said the ostrich, 'and my wife is called Cluster-of-Pearls.'

'Splendid names,' said Ali.

'Yes,' answered the bird, 'but goodness knows what we shall call the children. One of the most troublesome things about children is to know what to call them. They never like their names when they grow up and make them another grievance against their unfortunate father and mother.'

Mohammed walked beside them for a mile or two and grew a little brighter after Ali had given him a dozen dates. They told him where they lived, and he promised that he would come to see them some day and bring Cluster-of-Pearls.

'She is a good wife as wives go,' he said, 'but too cheerful and hopeful. Nothing casts her down, and to live night and day with an intensely hopeful person is depressing in itself.'

'If you can't cast her down, nobody could,' said Ben Josef.

Mohammed asked them their business presently.

'If it is not a rude question,' he said, 'what are you both doing here all alone without a caravan?'

'We are going to the Cliff of the Simoom,' answered Ali.

'Then stop at once,' begged the ostrich. 'Very lucky you met me. In fact you may thank me here and now for saving your lives, for the Cliff of the Simoom is death to everything and everybody. A thousand dreadful demons live there, and not so much as a white ant, or desert rat, would go within a mile of the place. So turn instantly and consider yourselves as deeply in my debt.'

But Ali explained to Mohammed that they were going on a great mission and could not turn back.

'It is a place of danger, no doubt,' he said, 'but there are no demons – only Nature at work.'

'No demons!' cried Mohammed. 'My dear young man, the place fairly swarms with demons – the deadliest demons in the desert – the demons of the poison wind!'

'Have you ever seen one?' asked Ali. 'Be honest, Mohammed, and tell the truth.'

'No,' answered the ostrich, 'I have never seen one, because I take very good care never to go near the horrid place.'

'Then how do you know they swarm there?' inquired the White Camel.

'Because they do,' replied Mohammed. 'Everybody

knows they do, and what everybody knows must be true.'

'Have you ever seen anybody who saw the demons?' asked Ali.

'I have not,' admitted Mohammed, 'but you can easily understand why. If you are near enough to see a demon, then, of course, you are near enough for him to see you. And once he sees you, you're done for and can never tell anybody about it. That's what they call logic.'

'We shall go all the same,' said Ali, and Mohammed prepared to leave them.

'Then you are a pair of idiots,' he answered, 'and I have done with you. There is not much society here and we welcome strange faces as a rule; but I am not going to be seen walking and talking with a pair of idiots. So I'll wish you goodbye; and when you meet the demons, remember my words. But it will be too late then.'

'Come and visit us at the oasis and we'll tell you what happened,' shouted Ali; but Mohammed was already gone, running on huge legs back to his home, with feathers fluttering in the wind as he tore along.

'What's wrong with him, I wonder?' said Ali.

'Nothing whatever,' answered Ben. 'He just grouses like that for fear people should know what a lucky chap he is.'

Chapter X

◆

The Adventure of the Simoom

A curious change came over the weather as Ali and Ben Josef travelled onwards and both felt that something very strange and very new and rather dreadful was going to happen. The sun burning over their heads seemed to grow tired and sulky. There were no clouds to dim his face, and they would have felt glad enough if there had been, but the air became heavy-laden and little puffs of wind cast up sudden twirls and twists of sand from the great billows of the desert over which the White Camel strode along. Then the clean glare of the sun turned into a sort of sickly colour and wisps of thin vapour, like turning serpents, began to writhe upon the sky. A far-off murmur also fell upon their ears – a sad and moaning sound that as yet came from somewhere a long way distant.

Both boy and beast were conscious of some great event about to happen in the desert and it made them uneasy; but neither was afraid. The White Camel marched stoutly forward, though the strange and lurid sky above him grew thicker and gloomier and the sun ceased to cast any shadow upon the sand.

'I think, Ali,' he said, 'that we are in for something pretty bad. Storms are of many kinds upon the desert and I have seen serious ones before today; but the sky never looked so strange to me as now, and I do not much like that queer sound booming away in front of us.'

'We must hope for the best,' answered his rider. 'You have gone fast, Ben, and we should be at the Cliff of the Simoom before very long.'

'We shall be,' answered Ben Josef, 'and if the coming storm holds up long enough, we may find some shelter under the precipices of the Cliff.'

After they had gone another couple of miles Ben cried out to Ali that their goal was in sight.

'You cannot see it yet seated on my hump,' he said, 'but when I lift my head, I mark a low, ink-black line cutting the desert like a knife. That is the famous Cliff of the Simoom, and an uglier sight I never wish to see.'

But both Ben and his rider were going to see something much uglier than the scowling ridge of rocks now heaving higher before them as they approached. Soon Ali could note the place, too, and when they had come within a mile of it, they saw that the beetling cliffs were a least two hundred feet high in some places, but cleft and ragged and torn here and there by past storms and tempests. Many great rocks had been flung down from them into the desert, but they were all as black as coal and not a ray of light, or streak of colour, shone upon the stern face of the precipice.

And then, as they stood still a moment to gaze upon this gloomy scene before proceeding to it, the sky darkened swiftly and the snaky vapours grew thicker until they hid the sun altogether. It seemed as though he were frightened and had fled out of the sky to escape. The light grew very dim and ashen, until, quite suddenly, a fearful sight appeared and the wanderers knew what was going to happen to them.

The strange noise increased, like the angry humming of a thousand wasps, and the sand began to fly into the air and sting their faces, for fierce puffs of wind accompanied the sound. But it was hotter than any wind either of them had ever felt before, and Ali expected every moment that he and Ben would catch fire from it.

Then over the black cliffs there rose up a huge, violet mass of cloud, like an enormous purple egg, and round about it flickered blue lightning dazzling bright. The day had grown quite dark now, as though night were about to fall, but the violet egg rolled on and the blue lightning streamed out of it and the fiery, savage wind roared louder and louder.

'What is going to happen?' asked Ben Josef. 'If we could tell what it was coming over the Cliff, I should know if there is anything to be done about it.'

And Ali told him what it was, for though he had never seen one, his father had told him about it.

CHAPTER X

'A simoom is upon us, Ben,' he said, 'and that is the most awful thing that can overtake men and beasts in the Red Desert. A simoom is like a cyclone in a way; but more terrible. Both are raging tempests against which neither man nor ship can do very much, and both have a centre of perfect calm in the midst of their rage and fury. A ship may ride peacefully on still water in the very midst of a mad cyclone, and a camel may lie at peace while a simoom roars and rages round him; but the difference is this. There is no immediate evil at the cyclone's heart; but at the simoom's heart is death. It is Samiel – the poison wind – and it were better to be in the thunder and lightning and horror of the thing itself than caught in that awful stillness within. For no living thing can breathe there.'

'Very interesting,' answered Ben. 'So now we know where we are. I didn't understand what was going to happen, but my dear mother, Morgiana, lived through a simoom in her time and taught me exactly what to do if ever I got into one. So jump off my back, Ali, and we will make ready and hope to be spared.'

'We have no time to reach the Cliff now,' answered Ali, 'and must face it here.'

He alighted and Ben Josef told him what was to be done.

'It takes about ten or twelve minutes for the simoom to sweep over any spot,' he said, 'and very soon it is going to sweep over us, so we are bound to be in its poisonous heart for a time. What we must attempt is to live through it, and if we could stop breathing for ten minutes we should be all right; but we have got to breathe. Now the nearer we are to the sand, the purer the air will be, and camels know this, and when a simoom bursts upon them, they squat down and bury their heads under the sand as far as they can, so that the poisonous air at the heart of the simoom may not get into them. You must do the same. Now rend your cloak and tie one half over your head and face, and tie the other half over my head and face; then we will both lie side by side as flat as we can, and when the simoom reaches us, burrow into the sand and breathe as little as possible and hope for the best.'

Ben had to shout his directions very loud, for the noise was now terrific and the thunder bellowed furiously and crashed upon the black cliffs so that they echoed its roar and were swiftly swallowed up in the purple mass of the simoom and vanished within it. But from behind the darkness there came one perfectly terrific sound, as though a thousand cannons had been fired together, and the ears of Ali and Ben Josef throbbed terribly to hear it.

'Some awful thing has happened on the Cliff,' bawled Ben. 'That was a different sound from all the others.'

'Don't shout,' begged Ali. 'Keep all your breath so that you can live when your head is under the sand.'

He tore his robe in half and wrapped one part very carefully round the White Camel's mouth and nostrils and eyes, and then Ben squatted down and pressed his neck into the sand and Ali covered his own head also. He flung himself close beside Ben Josef and as the hurricane burst upon them in clouds of stinging sand, plunged down his head and buried it and lay quite still. For a time there was nothing but burning wind that made both of them feel as though their limbs had turned into molten metal and caused them much pain; but then came the still, awful, poisonous heart of the simoom upon them and they strove to hold their breath in the moments of greatest danger. Ali wondered of many things as the minutes passed and thought of his mother and father and Morning Star and Sheikh Khalid and Seyf and Buz and Rupert and Abdullah and Mohammed and Jameel. And he wondered most why Jameel, if he knew about the simoom, had sent him and Ben Josef bang into it. He felt something like fire stealing down his throat and then mourned for Ben Josef and feared that he must be quite dead by now.

'He has such a tremendously long throat,' thought Ali, 'that it will be much worse for him than me.'

He had long lost all sense of time and could not guess whether he had been hidden in the sand five minutes, or five hours; but he dared not move though his lungs were bursting for a breath of pure air. Then he felt something dragging him up from the sand and thought this was another trick of the simoom, to pull him out and finish him. But it was only Ben Josef. Animals have a very good notion of time, and Ben made no mistake. He knew when the danger was over, and now he and Ali lay quite still together, just breathing the innocent, sweet, desert air into themselves and feeling the fire that had burned their limbs slowly ebb away. Ben was very silent for a long time and Ali went to their little store of food and brought him water to drink, for he was thirsty himself and thought that the White Camel would surely be. But Ben Josef felt no thirst or hunger for anything but air.

Far behind them the simoom sped away, and the red light of the setting sun came out and blazed upon its violet fringes.

'A close call, Ali,' said Ben, 'but here we are still. And here we will stop till morning. If we can sleep for many hours, that is the best for us both.'

'You shall sleep and I will keep watch,' answered Ali. 'It may come back.'

But his friend felt sure the simoom was gone for good, and soon they were both sound asleep under the stars in the peace and calm of the desert night.

They wakened not until the sun had risen over the black Cliff, and Ali wondered what they should do next.

'Have some breakfast,' said Ben. 'I never feel a day has fairly started until I get a nibble at something.'

They had brought food and a good bunch of Ben's beloved spurge, and while they ate, Ali wondered yet again why Jameel had ordered this plan of action.

'Nothing can come of it,' he said. 'How shall my father and the clan be any better for our dreadful adventure and narrow escape from death?'

'The old dreamer warned us that we were in for dangerous doings,' answered Ben Josef. 'But that was not all. He told us to go to the Cliff of the Simoom, and we have not been there yet. When we get there, we shall understand why he sent us.'

'I have seen all I ever want to see of the hideous place; but of course you are right and we must go there,' replied Ali; so, when their meal was eaten, he mounted and they made a start. Both were rather stiff and sore after the buffet of the storm, and they said but little as they went forward.

Now the Cliff, blacker than ever against the glory of the morning sky, towered above them grim and lifeless.

'It is an utterly poisonous place,' cried Ali. 'And well it may be, for it is the very home of Simoom. Here he dwells and breeds his dreadful poisons, so that not a herb, or beast, or bird can live within a mile of him.'

'He is gone for the present at any rate,' said Ben, 'and the air is cool and wholesome. Something happened here in the hurricane. You remember the terrific noise that nearly stunned us. We ought to be able to find out what it was, for such a fearful sound must mean a smash of some sort.'

They walked along the desolate sand strewn with rocks and boulders that had fallen from above, and after they had tramped a mile, the reason for what they had heard lay before them. Vast masses of rock had been torn from the cliffs and now cumbered the valley beneath. Fragments of the inky stone, as large as big houses, were flung down and the sand below was ploughed up and torn by the fall of them.

'The lightning must have struck and hurled the cliff down,' said Ali. 'In many places it beetles over and threatens to fall, and the lightning chose this spot and broke thousands of tons away.'

But Ben was thinking.

'This is surely the great thing that Jameel knew was going to happen,' he said. 'And still it is a mystery, for these fallen stones are of no use to anybody.'

They looked up at the naked surface of the cliff whence had poured this cataract of stones. It was of a tremendous blackness, but it had not been weathered by storm, or scorched by centuries of sunshine and, though dark enough, yet shone through its darkness and was brighter than the surrounding precipices. And then both Ali and Ben Josef saw something quite different, for all along the face of the new cliff there ran a dazzling thread of fire that glittered brilliantly by contrast with the gloom around it. The landslide had laid bare a sight such as they never saw before, and both stood silent and still, staring at it. Though this blazing rope of light running across the cliff face looked no more than a thread from beneath, in reality it was of some thickness. It wound about, now high now low, and extended for many yards along the broken face of the precipice.

'I cannot climb,' said Ben, 'but you can climb. You must seek a spot from which that glittering, yellow thread can be reached, and find what you make of it, for I have never seen the like on any hills of stone in the desert before.'

It proved not easy to reach a place where Ali could ascend and look into the matter; but he was a good climber, and presently he left Ben and made a perilous ascent upon the face of the cliff until he reached the shining band.

'Take care,' bade Ben Josef, 'for if you should fall and break your leg here, we shall be in a fix. What have you found?'

'I do not know,' shouted down Ali from his perch aloft. 'It seems to be a streak of solid clay almost as hard as metal, and it is deeply embedded upon the face of the rock. I will try to cut off a fragment with my knife and bring it to you. But I fear it is useless stuff.'

He set to work, for he always carried a knife, and presently he called out again.

'It is not very hard, but it is very heavy. It seems to be a sort of bright yellow lead.'

'Then I think I know what it is,' answered Ben, 'and if I am right, everything is explained and we can go home to Sheikh Heber as swiftly as possible.'

Ali jumped from rock to rock, rolled down one steep place and at last got back to the White Camel with his find. He held up two lumps of the yellow stuff and Ben knew in a moment what it was.

'This is gold!' he said. 'We have found a layer of gold running through the rock, and the simoom tore open this black precipice so that it should see the light and we should see it. We are the first creatures to see it, Ali. The gold has lain hidden here for millions of years, no doubt, yet so wise was Jameel that he knew it would leap out into the light of the sun today and sent us to find it.'

Ali was struck dumb at such a wonder and stared up at the ribbon of pure gold.

'How beautiful it is,' he said.

'It is one of those things that is both beautiful and useful,' answered Ben. 'But men do not waste much time admiring its beauty, because of its exceeding great usefulness. Gold is counted most precious of all metals and can be turned into everything you buy with money. But it is no use here. Your father will come with many camels and many men and convey it away as fast as possible.'

'It brings a sparkle of joy into this black wilderness,' said Ali. 'The dark cliffs have waited thousands of bitter years for one ray of light to shine upon their foreheads, and now their patience is rewarded and they are crowned with pure gold and become the wonder as well as the terror of the desert. It were cruel, Ben, to tear it away from them in their hour of triumph!'

'There are times when poetry does not seem to fit a situation,' answered Ben Josef, 'and this is one of them.'

He knelt down.

'Jump up quickly,' he commanded, 'and we will put in one of my famous sprints for home. We are exactly seventy miles from the oasis, and I ought to be there in twelve hours or a little less.'

'My father may think as I do and feel it an evil thing to rob the Cliff of the Simoom,' said Ali as they set off; but Ben only uttered a queer, gurgling sound which was his way of laughing.

'Your father knows of a great many empty stomachs,' he answered, 'and many acres of starving land crying for seed. Gold is more precious in the marts of gold just now for Sheikb Heber and his dear people – camels included – than on the dark forehead of Simoom's hateful home.'

So Ali ceased to argue about it and they sped forward till night fell. Then they rested for half an hour and ate the remainder of their food. The stars sailed over them and sank into the desert again and dawn broke and the sun arose. And still Ben kept his steady pace until the twinkle of the oasis shone out upon the sand once more and they were home again.

CHAPTER X

Whereupon Ali ran swiftly to his father's house and Ben strode off to tell Light of Day that he was safe and sound. And he drank a great drink and then went to sleep for twelve hours.

Chapter XI

♦

The Adventure of the Black Camel

Sheikh Heber told Ali of a good thing which had pleased him much while his son was away. He spoke first, and the young man listened to his father before he unfolded his own story.

'The dwarf,' said Heber, 'on one of his solitary rambles fell in with our neighbours and let them learn of our distress. Sheikh Khalid has also suffered from the locusts, but not as we have suffered, and when he heard that we were hungry and in sad want for ourselves and our stock, he set out himself and came with the best gifts in his power to bring. He brought good measure of grain for us and fodder for the beasts and, best of all, he brought friendship and sympathy and understanding. Would that it were in my power to repay him for this great and generous kindness, and much I hope that in time to come it may be.'

'If what Ben Josef says is true,' replied Ali, 'it will be in your power to repay him sooner than you think, Father. Tell me, please, the name of these lumps of metal that I have brought from the Cliff of the Simoom.'

Heber looked at Ali's great find and said that Ben was right.

'But this is solid gold!' he said. 'Whenever was it known the black Cliffs held gold?'

Then he heard the whole story and, of course, took it very seriously indeed.

'This is a tremendous happening,' declared Sheikh Heber, 'and there must be enough gold there to make me the richest sheikh in the Red Desert. Not that I have the least wish to be that, for gold brings its own cares, Ali. It often proves very difficult and disappointing stuff to manage. To get riches is easy if Allah wills, but to use them properly when you have them, is a very different matter. But I shall not shirk the challenge.'

Heart's Delight was thankful to see her son back again and horrified to hear his adventure and the thing that Jameel had told him to do; but she did not think the gold would be half so difficult as her husband imagined.

'It will be soon enough to worry about that when we have got it,' she said. 'As yet we know nothing. There may be but little there after all; but if there should be more than we want, few things are easier to give away. I never heard of anybody who had enough.'

Next morning Sheikh Heber and some of his wisest men set off with Ali to test the find and see, if possible, how deep this ribbon of gold might be; and they took with them Heber's copper-smith, a very skilful Arab in everything to do with metal. His name was Zaal. But Ben Josef did not go, as he was not yet rested.

The expedition remained absent for a week, and when it returned Heber told the clan of their good fortune, for Zaal had explored the rift of gold from end to end and discovered that there were many hundredweights clinging to the face of the rock – and not difficult to dig out.

There was no great fear that other wandering clans would find it, because the place had such a bad name; but nothing makes people braver than the promise of much gold, and Sheikh Heber found that the whole of his company – men and women and children – were all quite ready and willing to brave the peril if they could share the reward.

Before setting out to gather in the gold, however, Sheikh Heber did two wise things. He told his people to say nothing about this grand discovery for the present, because news flies on invisible wings in the desert, and until the gold was safe, the less said about it the better. And the second thing he did was to send two trusty messengers on camels to the nearest city, far away northward, where he had men of business who knew him and valued him and would understand what to do next. He felt safe now and in a position to order all that the clan wanted for its immediate needs, so the two messengers carried letters to many traders of the city, and Heber bade these merchants get together and fit out a caravan and bring him food and grain and supplies in general. He made them understand that money was no object at all and the quicker they came and the more rich supplies they brought, the better he would be pleased and the better they would be paid.

And then he chose one hundred and twenty strong men and eighty camels – the best that were left – and set out once more for the treasure. Zaal came to direct the workers and see if there was yet more gold to be found, and Ali came with Ben Josef, because Ben was far the strongest camel of them all and would be able to bring a good load back. A strong, healthy camel can carry two hundredweight of load, but Sheikh Heber's camels were thin and not very strong now, owing to the famine, and he could not ask them to carry anything like two hundredweight at present. But Ben knew that he was still good for two hundredweight if necessary.

They brought ropes and picks and tents with them and set their camp in a sheltered spot. Water was the difficult problem, for it would be impossible to stay at work on the cliffs for very long without it. But Seyf, who went with the expedition, found a spring beneath a great rock not more than a mile from the cliff, and though the water was brackish and a little salty, yet it proved wholesome and abundant.

The work went on steadily, and the Arabs, though they had never done anything like this before, did not mind being lowered with ropes to the face of the cliff. They used their picks as Zaal taught them, and cut out the gold in chunks, while below it was gathered up and stored and guarded. Then, as the vein of gold began to run dry, and Zaal said that two more days of work would finish it, Sheikh Heber dispatched Seyf back to the oasis and directed him to return with another hundred of the strongest men left there. They were to come armed and mounted on horses, because when the gold started over the lonely desert, it would have to be protected from any robbers who might roam that way, or have heard what Heber's people were doing.

Zaal at last declared that though more gold might still be hidden in the heart of the black cliff, it would need another simoom to lay it bare; while Heber thought when he looked at the tons of yellow metal now waiting to be carried away, that he must be the richest person the world had ever known. But he was wrong there. He had certainly won a very large fortune, however – more than enough to make him anxious.

The fighting men arrived, armed to the teeth with spears and swords and guns, and after a night's rest the business of packing the gold on to the camels began.

'The first thing I shall do after getting home,' said Sheikh Heber to Ali, 'will be to send a mighty good load of this stuff to my friend, Khalid. He looks at gold as highly desirable, and I feel sure it will not worry him to receive a ton or two of it.'

'We might get Zaal to make some lovely works of art out of it,' said Ali. 'You cannot give money to everybody, and gold, after all, is only another name for money; but you can give anybody a lovely cup, or salver of rare workmanship, and they would delight to take it.'

'Sheikh Khalid is what they call a realist,' replied Heber. 'He will make no difficulty, and though he is proud enough for anything, when he hears how I have come by the gold, he will say "Kismet!" and accept as much as I am pleased to give him. Quite right, too!'

'There is the dear dreamer, Jameel, to be thought upon,' continued Ali. 'Gold is no good to him indeed, but beauty is very good to him, and Zaal shall make two things of rare beauty, which he will rejoice to do, for he loves to make them when he can spare time from hammering the pots and pans. Two rare, fine things he shall create out of the gold, and I will carry one to Jameel when I go to tell him of the blessings he has brought us.'

'And where will you carry the other?' asked Sheikh Heber.

'I will carry the other to Sheikh Khalid's daughter, Morning Star,' said Ali.

They came back safely by easy stages, and Heber breathed again to know the treasure safe. All he now wanted was to see a rich caravan from the north, and presently it came and the first smile for many long months lighted the sheikh's dark eyes as he watched his flocks and herds eating their fill once more. The husbandmen soon set to work sowing corn and crops and planting fresh coffee-shrubs and orange-trees; and the date-palms, that had looked so wretched, began to put forth new fronds and clothe their ragged heads with foliage again.

With the caravan came wise and trusty men who understood gold and declared that the treasure was the purest gold such as they had seldom seen before.

But Sheikh Heber had set aside five tons for Sheikh Khalid and he said nothing about that. They decided that when all his expenses had been paid and the gold brought safely to the strongholds of the city in the north, Sheikh Heber would have several million of money for his own; and they hoped that he would now turn his back on the desert and come and live a civilized life among houses and set to work to turn each million into two million, if not three. They tried to explain what a million means exactly, and what a million can do in the world if properly managed by people who understand how to make money breed money; but Heber laughed at them and said that if he had to pay every penny for permission to go on living his desert life, he would do so.

'What of my people and my flocks and my oasis?' he said. 'Shall I leave these things for the stuffy palace and the scents and scenes of a great city?'

So they saw that it was no good trying to knock sense into him, but taught him how to write cheques and do accounts and pay taxes and so on, and promised to sell his gold and invest the money. They were honest men and he trusted them, and they said that they would send him caravans from time to time laden with every delight of civilization, including a radio with television, so that he could see all the joys he was missing. Then he thanked them and feasted them to the best of his power, and they all went home to the great city and were jolly glad to get back to it.

Of course the clan was very excited about their increased importance and every man and woman looked at the gold from their own point of view. The women saw it turning into bracelets and necklaces

and ear-rings, to make a sweet tinkle about them as
they moved along; and the men saw it turning into
land and fresh fields and Arab horses and noble
young beasts. Sage Omar rushed to his books to read
all about gold and how Nature made it, which was
the only interest it had for him, and Heart's Delight
planned gifts of every sort for the clan and their children. Seyf prayed for a new camel, and Zaal, the coppersmith, begged to make some beautiful things.
Indeed he set about them very soon when gold was
given him. He fashioned a big bowl of fine and simple workmanship for Jameel, and he also made a very
lovely drinking vessel at Ali's wish.

When this exquisite cup was ready, Ben Josef and
his master started for the camp of Sheikh Khalid, and
Ben helped many other camels to carry the present
that Heber was sending to his friend. They set off in
good spirits for a three days' march.

Ali told of a mighty resolve as they tramped along
with the string of camels and their escort. He alighted
sometimes and walked, to lessen Ben Josef's burden,
and while he walked, he revealed the thing that he
was going to do.

'It will surprise you to hear, Ben,' he said, 'that I
am going to ask Sheikh Khalid's daughter, Morning
Star, to marry me.'

'Not in the least,' answered the White Camel. 'I
have known that you were going to do so for ages.'

'Nothing ever seems to surprise you,' answered
Ali.

'I hope she'll like you as well as I do,' answered
Ben.

'I have not told my parents,' continued Ali,

'because, if she refuses, they would be sorry for me. So nobody need know but you. It is not very likely hat she will care about me. Indeed, she may already be promised to some much more important chap than I am.'

'We must hope for the best,' said Ben.

And when at last they came to the encampment of Khalid's people and he hastened to welcome them, Ali told him the news and gave him a message from Sheikh Heber.

'My father sends you greeting and blessing,' he said, 'and since Allah has smiled upon him, it becomes his duty and joy to smile upon other people as quickly as possible. He has sent you a little gift of solid gold.'

Khalid smiled and showed pleasure. He thought that Heber had probably sent him a ring, or a match-box, or some trifle of that sort. But Ali went on.

'This present is not a return for your precious gift to my father,' he said, 'because no man can return a gift. That were a base thought, and your timely and splendid kindness to Sheikh Heber can never be returned. But the goodwill behind it and the friend-ship that made you come to help him in his need can be echoed, and the greatest delight my father felt at his fortune was to think that you might share it. He said that out of your generosity he trusted you would accept this gift, though a lesser thing than your own.'

'I shall certainly accept it if it were but a grain of gold,' said Khalid.

'It is five tons of pure gold,' answered Ali; and when Khalid heard that the young man had brought five tons, he feared for him.

'You have been in the sun too long, boy,' he said. 'Your wits are spinning. One does not talk of gold as though it were dates, or corn.'

But there was the gold all right, and Khalid did not hesitate to accept it.

'We are made men,' he said, 'and there shall be friendship between your people and my people and they shall become as brothers and sisters, with good-willing and trust in all their hearts for each other.'

That night, when he sat alone with Khalid and his son Salem, Ali told of his great hope.

'I want to marry Morning Star,' he said in his direct fashion. 'It is not very likely that she will want to marry me, I fear; but at any rate I can ask her, if you will allow me to do so and would like me for another son.'

'I should dearly like you for a brother,' declared Salem.

'I have given her the drinking vessel made of gold,' said Ali, 'and she smiled upon it and was glad. And she smiled upon me, too, and said that she rejoiced that I had come. But, of course, there is a good deal of difference between rejoicing to see a person and marrying them.'

But Sheikh Khalid frowned, and Ali feared that he was going to forbid him to make love to Morning Star.

'There is one rather sad, serious difficulty for you,' he began presently. 'My daughter has already lis-tened to many suitors, for her loveliness can no more be hid than the star after which she is named; but no young man has ever been such as she could wish to wed, and she has been cunning and always made a condition to put them off. It is well known that she will never marry anybody who cannot give her a black camel. And she made this promise, because such a beast is rarer than frost in the desert. A white camel, such as your great Ben Josef, is exceedingly rare, and until I had seen him and watched his awful fighting, as though ten demons drove him on, I never believed such a mighty creature could exist; but one has sometimes heard of snow-white camels. I have, however, never in all my life met with a really black camel, and it is very doubtful if such a thing ever existed; so when Morning Star made that a condition of marriage, the young men began to fall off pretty quickly, because they knew there is certainly no such camel to be met with in the Red Desert, or any other desert. But a promise is a promise, and even though she found that she could love you, Morning Star will never depart from her solemn word.'

Ali did not sleep very well that night, though he was cheered up next day when he asked Morning Star to marry him.

'I have heard about the black camel,' he said, 'and you must keep your word; yet there is more to be spoken. There may or may not be a black camel in the world, and if there isn't, that is an end to the matter. But, first, I must know what would happen if I found a black camel?'

'If such a thing were in the world and you found it, I would surely marry you,' answered Morning Star, 'because I love you very much indeed, and I loved you the first time I saw you, for there is nobody like you. And because there is such a rare and wonderful boy in the world as you are, then there may be such a rare and wonderful camel as a black camel.'

'To know you love me is the first grand thing,' said Ali, 'and to find a coal-black camel is the second grand thing. And if I can't do it, then I am not worthy of you.'

'Try,' begged Morning Star. 'You are so clever that I believe, if you try hard enough, you will find one.'

'I will certainly roam the round earth to find one,' he promised. 'The camel people are a mighty host, and though Sheikh Khalid has never seen a black one and, until yesterday, I had never heard of such a thing, yet even such a camel there may be; and if there is, I will find it.'

'I shall make my brother and my father and all the clan look too,' she promised. 'I love you so very much, Ali, that it would be a most dreadful grief for me not to be your wife some day.'

As they travelled homeward, Ali talked to Ben and told him what must be done; but the White Camel did not feel very hopeful about it from the first.

'I don't believe there is such a thing,' he said, 'and if there isn't such a thing, then she ought not to feel bound to keep her word.'

'Haven't you ever heard of a black camel?' asked Ali.

'Often,' answered Ben; 'but we hear of plenty of things that nobody has ever seen, or ever will see.'

'The question in my mind is where to begin hunting,' said Ali. 'We must make a start as quickly as we can.'

'I quite understand that,' replied Ben, 'but there ought to be a bargain. If there is no such thing, then you can't find it; but you must not go on hunting till your hair turns white and Morning Star is an old lady.

You ought to say to her, "If I hunt for – say five years – and fail, will you agree that there are no black camels and so feel free to marry me?"'

But Ali shook his head.

'It is a black camel or nothing,' he answered. 'There may be no such beast, but if there is no such beast, yet there will be enough of such a beast to come between us for ever.'

'People ought to be careful how they talk,' said Ben Josef. 'To say a silly thing is an everyday matter; but if Morning Star is going to stick to it afterwards; then you may both be sadly disappointed and unhappy for the rest of your lives.'

Ali did not answer, but Ben had another idea which cheered him a little.

'We are going next week,' he said, 'to set out for ancient Jameel and carry him your father's gratitude and the golden bowl that Zaal has made for him. You shall tell your story to the Dreamer and see if he can do anything about it. He is so amazingly wise that he may know some way to get you out of this scrape.'

'He might dream a way out,' thought Ali. 'He puts his trust in dreams and told us that his have a way of always coming true.'

Before very long the young man set off again with Ben Josef to visit Jameel, and once more they found that he was expecting them and ready to make them welcome. He also knew all about their adventure in the simoom and how they had discovered the rift of gold. Six months were past since they had seen him, but he was not changed and treated them kindly and graciously.

They arrived at sundown, and after they had eaten

and drunk, and Ali had spoken of the past, told that things now promised very hopefully for Sheikh Heber and his people, and reported his father's everlasting gratitude, he let Jameel hear his own story, and how he loved Morning Star and was loved by her, but the black camel had come between.

'Wit of man,' said Ali, 'cannot find a way out of this hopeless fix, dear Jameel; but Ben Josef reminded me that if there were a way, you would know it.'

Jameel was holding his gift of the golden bowl, which had given him much pleasure. He admired the rare skill that had gone to make it and said:

'There is only one greater joy than mine in this work of art, and that is the joy of the artist who made it. Of this gold at least we may say that it has been put to good uses and fashioned by the craft of Zaal into a precious thing. Be sure to tell him I think it is a grand piece of work and know that only a great artist could have made it.'

Then he answered Ali's story, but had not very much to say.

'Your case is indeed difficult,' he said, 'for the reason that there is no black camel in the world; but often these knotty problems may be solved if we tackle them in the right spirit. At any rate Morning Star is exceedingly right to stick to her word, and you must not try to make her break it. As you know, my thoughts are largely directed by my dreams, and I hope tonight that a good dream may come to help you.'

They soon went to bed, and when the sun rose again and the time for breakfast was come, Ali longed to hear if Jameel had dreamed anything helpful; but of course he waited until the old man mentioned the subject, and then it was only to hear that no dream at all had visited the hermit.

'But do not feel disappointed,' said Jameel. 'A dream will surely come in a night or two. One never knows for certain when it will visit one. And you must be brave and prepare to hear that nothing can be done for you and that you can do nothing for yourself. Such is often man's hard fate. But we will live in hope.'

'You cannot suggest any plan yourself, dear Jameel?' asked Ali, and the ancient man confessed that he could not.

On the third night of their stay, however, Jameel dreamed a dream, and he was cheerful at breakfast next morning and told Ben Josef and Ali about it. He himself seemed very pleased at what he had dreamed; but his hearers could not find much to be pleased about, for it seemed to both of them that Jameel's dream was nonsense.

'Now listen to me,' began the hermit after he had eaten three dates and drunk a little water; and at first he did not speak of Ali, but rambled on in his usual fashion.

'Last night I dreamed as follows. I dreamed that the future belongs to those who have pluck to face it,' he said, 'and I am rather astonished to find how few people do face the future. There are rather more than two thousand millions of people in the world, and most of them are doubtless worrying a good deal about the future; but very few are facing it, or teaching their children how to face it. Young people want to be somebody and do something when they grow up; but the grand thing for them to find out is not so much what they want to do, but what they are most likely to do best. Idiots tell us that the future will look after itself, whereas nothing really wants looking after more. Ours is the present, and the best that we can do with it is to work and plan for those who will follow us and inherit the future.

'Now this will not interest you at all,' proceeded Jameel; 'but from it arose your affair, and there came into my mind the thought that you and Ben are a plucky pair who face the future in the right spirit. So I spoke to the Shadow, who was with me in my dream, and told him that you were a brave lad and in love; but I also told him that you were in great difficulty, yet willing to face any trouble and danger if you could conquer your fix. Whereupon the Shadow answered thus. "When approaching a tough problem, friend," he said, "always remember that there are two main roads by which it may be tackled: the road of Reason and the road of Faith. Thus you will have two strings to your bow, for if Reason declares that there is no way out of a mess and the problem cannot be solved by Reason, then Faith may come to the rescue and do the trick. Reason may kill hope; Faith may bring it to life again."

'And then,' said Jameel, 'the Shadow told me exactly what I was to tell you, and I saw clearly what he meant when he spoke of Reason and Faith. This is all that has to be said, Ali, and you must make what you can of it.'

He stopped and then uttered these curious words.

'There is no black camel in the world; but a black camel will be at the oasis of Sheikh Heber when Ali gets home again.'

The lad stared at Jameel.

'Can you make any sense of that?' he asked.

'Certainly I can,' replied the hermit. 'It is most interesting and I understand it very well indeed.'

'How can Reason, or Faith, or anything else, make sense of it?' asked Ali. 'If there isn't a black camel in the whole world, dear Jameel, how in the name of Allah can there be one waiting for me at the oasis?'

'The simplest way will be to go home and find out,' said Ben Josef, and the hermit Jameel agreed with Ben.

'Use your reason as you go,' he said, 'and if that can't show you what the dream meant, then give Faith a chance and believe in me.'

So they left the little green nest in the porphyry hills, where the old man lived, and set off again for home. But Ali was a good deal cast down and took rather a hopeless view of the situation.

'There must be some sense in what he said,' argued Ben Josef. 'It certainly doesn't make sense to you or me, but it made sense to him, therefore there must be sense hidden in it.'

'From the point of view of reason there is no sense and can be none,' answered Ali. 'What Jameel said is something they call a contradiction in terms, Ben, and half his speech is flatly contradicted by the other half. Both things he told us can't be true, and not all the reasoning and arguing on earth could make them both true. This blessed Shadow he talks about says that there is no such thing as a black camel in the world. That's clear enough and, no doubt, only too true. And then, in the very same breath, we are told that we shall find a black camel when we get back to the oasis.'

'I grant you it beats our reasoning powers,' admitted Ben Josef. 'Reason can't make top or tail of it, as they say, so now let us see if Faith is any use. Faith means believing in something that can't be proved by reason – at any rate not by the sort of reason given to men and camels. We beasts have, of course, to take a great deal on faith, and I do not find it difficult myself; but you always wanted to get to the bottom of everything and never liked taking other people's opinions on faith.'

'If you are given reasoning powers, you ought to use them,' answered Ali; 'but in this case there is no reason, nor rhyme either, in what I have been told.'

'Then try if you can bring Faith to work on it,' advised Ben.

'Faith in what?' asked Ali. 'You can't put any faith in a contradiction in terms.'

'Jameel is not a contradiction in terms,' answered the White Camel. 'We have to remember that Jameel thought the dream an excellent dream and felt quite satisfied with it. He knew what it meant, and he is far wiser than you are, or I can be. We ought to be bright enough to understand it.'

'No,' declared Ali. 'It is senseless; and I fear the only thing it can possibly mean is that dear old Jameel is losing his wits at last. If you live long enough, you always do. That's why they say an old man is a child again.'

'Old people don't lose their wits as completely as young people often think they have,' answered Ben Josef. 'I am getting on myself and shall soon be called old; but I have my wits in very good order still, and they tell me that Faith is the only thing for us to-day.

I trust Jameel, and I firmly believe that, though there may not be a black camel in the world, a black camel will none the less be waiting for you in the oasis.'

'You surprise me, Ben!' cried Ali.

'Nothing like a surprise if it is a pleasant one,' answered his friend.

Towards sunset on the third day of their return journey home, they marked the oasis glimmering in sunset light and were glad to be back again. Yet Ali felt very sad, and he calmed his mind with great thoughts of how he would search all the three Arabias for a black camel and never rest again until he had found one. But Ben was calm and satisfied, because Faith has a more restful effect on the nerves than Reason if you are a young man, or a middle-aged camel.

Then they saw a spot on the desert moving between them and home and marked a mounted man approaching them swiftly. Presently he came close, and there was Seyf, the dwarf, perched on his new camel and very proud of its paces. He looked tinier than ever on the top of the great, brown dromedary that Sheikh Heber had given him.

They welcomed him and he spoke.

'I knew that you would be back tonight,' he said, 'so I rode out to show you my grand new camel and tell you something very interesting that happened this morning.'

'Interesting to Ben Josef, or to me?' asked Ali.

'Most interesting for you both,' replied Seyf. 'Ben Josef is a proud father, for his wife, Light of Day, has given birth to a fine young male camel.'

'Is he white?' asked Ben.

Chapter XI

'No,' answered the dwarf. 'Not a white hair on him. Your son is as black as Satan.'

Chapter XII

◆

The Adventure of the Honeymoon

It was quite wrong of Seyf to say that Ben Josef's son appeared to be as black as Satan, because there are all kinds of blackness and the little camel could not be called that sort at all. He was certainly as black as the ace of spades, but it was a beautiful blackness; and if you want to know exactly what he looked like, find a piece of charcoal and you will see that over its gloomy colour is spread a beautiful silver; or if your mother happens to have a black pearl, then you will understand exactly what the little camel looked like all over. He grew out of this as he became older and in time to come was a glorious creature, as big as his father and as black as night; but that is how he began, and before Ben Josef came home and saw him, Light of Day had already called her son Black Pearl; and that was his name for evermore.

You can guess how excited Ali felt and how he longed to take the little camel to Morning Star; but he had to wait awhile before he could do that. He went to see her pretty quickly and she rejoiced to hear that a real black camel had been found for her and hoped that her wedding with Ali would not be long delayed. But these things take time and it was not until many moons had passed that Ali and Morning Star were married.

At first Light of Day did not at all like the thought of losing her son so quickly, but Ben Josef explained to her that Black Pearl would soon return to his family.

'When we are wed, Ali's wife will live with us,' he told her, 'and our son will come back with her. It is already settled that Black Pearl will carry Morning Star and nobody else when he is big and strong enough to do so.'

The arrival of the black camel made quite a sensation, and Arab people came from far to see it. Some rich men offered Ali thousands of pounds for Black Pearl, but of course he was not to be sold. Indeed he soon belonged to Morning Star, for presently Black Pearl marched along beside his father by easy stages and arrived in the camp of Sheikh Khalid. To see snow-white Ben Josef and his little black son walking together was a grand sight, and Ben told Ali that Black Pearl had unusually big feet already, which meant that, when he grew up, he would be an enormous camel, perhaps even greater than his father.

At last the marriage morn arrived, and Sheikh

The Adventure of the Honeymoon

Khalid made holiday and feasted Sheikh Heber and his great men in splendid fashion. It was a grand affair, and when the ceremony had ended and the banquets were all finished and the wedding presents had been admired and praised, Sheikh Khalid and his people went on their way to their haunts in the desert, and Sheikh Heber and his people set off once more for the Purple Mountains, and Ali and Morning Star went to spend their honeymoon at the oasis.

Many people think that honeymoons are dull and drag rather, because honeymooners are left all alone; and in high society nobody goes near them on any account; but there was no high society at the oasis, and Ali and Morning Star were never dull for a moment. Indeed, quite a number of unexpected visitors dropped in and then dropped out again.

And the first visitor was rather alarming and mysterious. Buz, the goat, told Ali one morning that very queer things were happening, for two of his grandchildren had disappeared and Buz felt much troubled about it.

'They were of no account' he said; 'still they ought not to have vanished without warning in this way.'

Nobody could explain the loss, and then, as he walked with Morning Star in his father's garden at noon on a cloudless day under the shade of the date-palms, Ali saw a huge object like a log lying on the grass, and feared that a tree had fallen, and wondered why. But a moment later he understood that it was no tree. Abdullah, the giant serpent, lay there, and the monster was stretched out sound asleep. In all his wonderful beauty he slumbered, and where the sunbeams fell between the fronds of the palms they flashed upon Abdullah's gorgeous coat of ebony and silver and scarlet and orange.

Morning Star, as soon as she saw the great snake, was frightened and turned to run away; but Ali called her back.

'Fear nothing,' he said. 'This is a personal friend of mine.'

'You have such funny friends, darling,' answered Morning Star; and then Ali wakened Abdullah and asked him how he was getting on and said he was glad to see him.

'I thought I'd just drop in for a change of scene and diet,' said Abdullah. 'I told you that I would come if I could make time, some day, and I did make time, and here I am. This is a very pleasant spot and I am quite enjoying myself so far.'

Ali introduced his wife, and Abdullah showed off and invited her to examine his exquisite pattern; but Morning Star said quite the wrong thing unfortunately, though of course she meant to say the right one.

'You are very like a magnificent Persian carpet that lies in my father's tent,' she said; but Abdullah's diamond eyes flashed, and he hissed rather sharply.

'Nobody should be compared to anybody else,' he answered. 'It is a poor compliment even to compare everyday, commonplace people with other commonplace people; but when you say that I put you in mind of anything else, you talk stupid nonsense, because there is nothing else in the world like me, and never was, and never will be.'

'I'm very sorry, Abdullah,' answered Morning Star. 'It was your lovely pattern that put me in mind of the carpet.'

'Absurd!' he replied. 'No carpet from Persia has a pattern like mine. My pattern came direct from Allah, and what weaver of carpets could do anything like this? You ought to have been dazzled and amazed, instead of trying to think of something like me, so do remember in future that there is nothing like me.'

Morning Star laughed, and Ali made a tactful remark.

'How lucky am I,' he said, 'to be with two peerless people at once! For I am sure there can be nothing in the world more lovely than either of you.'

'Girls are many,' replied Abdulah, 'but other snakes such as I are not merely few – they don't exist.'

'Well, enjoy yourself in your own way, my dear fellow,' replied Ali. 'I'm afraid we woke you from your dreams. No doubt we shall meet again.'

He was moving off; but Abdullah asked a very awkward question. 'Tell me,' he said, 'why your goats, instead of wandering about as usual, are all penned up together with a dozen hulking savage dogs to guard them? I ask because I am hungry this morning, and I thought, as a guest, that I should be free of everything you had.'

'You explain a mystery,' replied Ali. 'We were wondering where two young goats had gone.''

'You would surely not expect me to eat old goats, would you?' asked Abdullah.

'I'm afraid I must ask you not to eat any goats at all,' replied Ali. 'They are my father's goats and he wouldn't like it.'

The serpent was very angry to hear this.

'Do you call that hospitality?' he asked. 'Very well

then! I won't stop another minute! I never heard of such a mean, miserable welcome.'

'I saw a fine hare yesterday,' said Morning Star. 'Perhaps you could catch that, Abdullah.'

'I may love hares, and as a matter of fact I do; but you don't usually expect to be told to catch your meals when you are asked to a house-party,' he answered.

Then Ali, who did not think this was the way to talk to a lady, spoke rather sternly to Abdullah.

'This isn't a house-party,' he said. 'It's a honey-moon; and you can't say you were asked exactly. You told me you might come if you had nothing better to do; but evidently we don't suit you, so I think it would be well if we said good-bye.'

'You must not regard me as a friend any more then,' answered Abdullah, 'and I hope I shall never see either of you again. Your goats weren't up to much, either.'

'Well, good-bye, and a safe journey,' replied Ali. 'How is dear Jameel?'

'All the better for my friendship,' replied Abdullah. 'A pity you aren't more like him. He at least knows a gentleman when he meets one.'

Then the bad-tempered monster coiled and twisted and rolled away, and left Sheikh Heber's oasis, never to return.

'I always hated snakes,' declared Morning Star, 'and he hasn't made me feel any kinder to them.'

'I expect that it is living so much alone, poor fel-low,' thought Ali. 'He ought to have let us know that he was coming, and then we could have arranged something to please him.'

'Never invite him again,' begged Morning Star. 'It

is idle to arrange things to please people who are so pleased with themselves. He wasn't half as beautiful as my father's rug, really.'

'Yet he is very wise,' answered Ali.

'There is a lot of difference between being wise and thinking you are,' said Morning Star.

'At any rate he is gone, and we will turn our thoughts to happier people,' he told her.

'He said girls were many,' grumbled Morning Star. 'Fancy saying that to you!'

'There is only one girl in the whole world as far as I know,' said Ali.

On another day, when they rambled together on the fringes of the oasis, they came upon two ostriches poking about side by side, and Ali instantly recognized them.

'More friends!' he cried. 'Here's dear old Mohammed with his mate!'

'Is he a stuck-up pig like Abdullah?' asked Morning Star.

'Not a bit, a capital chap,' answered Ali. 'He warned me against the Cliff of the Simoom long ago and will be much surprised to find me still alive. He believes in demons and all sorts of things.'

On seeing Ali, the great plumed ostrich approached, and his wife, Cluster-of-Pearls, followed him.

'Welcome!' said Ali. 'Follow me into the cool of the oasis, both of you, and see what you can find to enjoy.'

'I am thankful to see you still alive,' replied Mohammed, 'but how you escaped the demons I cannot imagine.'

Then he heard all about it and walked with his friend under the palm-trees.

'This is my wife,' he said. 'She begged to come and I felt that, if you and the White Camel were still living, you would not mind.'

'Delighted to see both of you,' answered Ali. 'Your wife is evidently a very fine bird.'

'She's all right,' admitted Mohammed, 'and a good wife and mother. Of course we cannot choose our looks.'

'I think she's quite beautiful,' declared Morning Star. '

You can't possibly think that,' replied Mohammed, 'but don't suppose I am running her down – far from it. I married her for her amiable character, which after all is the thing that matters most.'

'How did the eggs hatch out?' asked Ali.

'Beautifully,' declared Cluster-of-Pearls. 'We have four sons and one daughter, and the boys take after their father and promise to be magnificent creatures, and the girl unfortunately takes after me.'

'We are hoping that she will outgrow it, however,' said Mohammed. 'A rare handful they are – just getting to the disobedient age – still people seem to admire them – I can't imagine why.'

'He is as proud of them as possible, really,' whispered Cluster-of-Pearls, 'and he knows perfectly well that they are magnificent children.'

Ali hoped the ostriches would enjoy themselves, and Mohammed asked a question as he looked at the oranges and pomegranates hanging on the boughs.

'What may we be allowed to eat without being greedy and rude?' he inquired.

'Anything you can reach,' answered Ali; and that was a pretty generous answer because Mohammed stood eight feet tall.

'A little fruit will be such a treat and do us much good,' said Cluster-of-Pearls; 'but you must not let us be in the way.'

'You won't be in the way,' promised Ali; and then, to show his gratitude, Mohammed twisted round his neck, plucked a magnificent, snow-white plume from his tail, bowed and presented it to Morning Star.

'A little memento of a happy occasion,' he said, 'and I venture to think you will not meet with a better feather in a hurry.'

'It is a grand gift,' answered Morning Star. 'I have never seen another to match it and I thank you very, very much, Mohamed.'

They left the ostriches, then, to amuse themselves in their own way, and a few days later, wandering in a dell of sweet grass, came suddenly upon a brown hare, nibbling heartily and making a big meal.

'Why!' cried Ali, 'there's that little liar, Rupert!'

'Another of your odd friends, darling?' asked Morning Star.

'Not a friend exactly, but an old acquaintance,' replied Ali, and Rupert, for it was indeed he, seeing that he could not well run away, sat up and lifted his front paws.

'Comrade!' he squeaked.

'How did you get here, Rupert?' asked Ali.

'How I get everywhere,' answered the hare: 'on my paws; but if I had no right to come, I will be off at once. I just saw an oasis as I was wandering round; but of course I didn't know it belonged to you.'

'It doesn't,' answered Ali, 'it belongs to my father. There is no objection to you having a good time here all the same; but I should like to ask you one question.

You very well remember that you promised to meet me again in a week after our last talk. You promised most faithfully to be there, and yet, when I came and called you, you never answered.'

Rupert looked rather nervous and brushed a few blades of grass off his face. His little brain was working hard, but he wanted time to think how to answer, so he asked a question himself.

'I do hope your dear mother recovered,' he said. 'I've been worrying about her ever since.'

'Thanks to the cleverness of Sage Tarik, the doctor, she quite recovered, I am glad to say,' answered Ali. 'So you needn't worry about her. But now, why did you break your word?'

'Well,' replied Rupert. 'I'll tell you exactly what happened. And I wouldn't go so far as to say I broke my word exactly. I grant you I did not keep the appointment, but, strictly speaking, it wasn't my fault. I had quite decided to be jugged for your dear mother, if the doctor agreed. You might almost say I wanted to be jugged for her and felt it would be a very praiseworthy end. But owing to a bit of bad luck, I missed you through no fault of my own.'

'How was that?' asked Ali.

'Well, I got a nasty touch of influenza,' replied Rupert. 'Honest to goodness I did. And when you came again I was pretty well down and out. I heard you call me, but hadn't the strength to answer. And my head was dreadful and I ached all over. And far worse than the influenza was the thought that you had probably come to kill me for your mother and there was I – much too ill to be shot. I never felt so disappointed in my life!'

'Of course you can't jug hare with influenza,' said Morning Star. 'But you recovered?'

'Yes – I got over it; though I wouldn't say that I have ever been quite the same hare since,' sighed Rupert. 'It was a nasty attack.'

'It may interest you to know that I had merely brought you a present,' said Ali. 'Tarik didn't want you for my mother; and to reward you for telling me about him, I had brought you some very pretty eating and a fine bunch of grapes.'

'To think of that!' gasped Rupert. 'And grapes the one thing I was longing for. Nothing like grapes for influenza. I see some grand bunches on your vines here, by the way.'

Ali looked at Rupert thoughtfully. He felt pretty certain that he had told a pack of lies; but he was a visitor, even though he had invited himself, and you can't very well accuse a visitor of telling stories.

'I should like to believe you, Rupert,' he said, 'and in any case you don't matter very much, because, as Ben Josef told me, nothing really matters. Here are some grapes, any way.'

He picked a bunch of fat, purple grapes from a vine, and Rupert's eyes glittered.

'You are a host in a thousand,' he said. 'I am now, of course, very old indeed, and the days of jugging are past for ever – which is one of the few advantages about growing old, if you are a hare; but I should love to make any other return in my power.'

'It is fortunate that you missed Abdullah,' said Morning Star. 'He told us that he loved hares.'

'And who may Abdullah be?' asked Rupert.

'A huge serpent,' she answered. 'He has only just left us.'

But Rupert was quite overcome at this dreadful news. He forgot his grapes and his manners and everything.

'Here – let me get out of this!' he squeaked. 'If there is a serpent about, then I'll push off at once – don't try to keep me.'

'We're not,' said Ali; 'but the great Abdullah has gone. He didn't like us.'

'He may come back,' answered Rupert. 'The one thing a snake always does is what you don't expect him to do. In fact I'll bet anything he'll come back. I've had some very narrow shaves from the hateful brutes in my time and they've eaten dozens of my relations.'

He was trembling and looking almost as mad as a March hare.

'Which is the nearest way out of this place?' he asked. 'I want to hop it at once.'

Ali pointed, and in a moment Rupert was off like an arrow without even stopping to say good-bye.

'A good bunch of grapes wasted,' said Morning Star. 'What a little coward he was!'

Ali picked up the grapes and gave them to a passing goat.

'Rupert is as Allah made him, I'm afraid,' he answered. 'And cowards are often liars too. Lies are the most trustworthy weapon for a coward, and hares, being timid by nature, are rather apt to draw the long bow, no doubt. We can only hope that he won't run into Abdullah on the way home.'

'I wonder which of your funny friends will turn up next?' asked Morning Star; but nobody else of any importance appeared, and their chief interest outside themselves was the growing son of Ben Josef. He began to be a magnificent camel, and was docile and very friendly from the first. He followed Morning Star about like a great dog, and she wondered how long it would be before he was big enough to ride. But Ali noticed one thing about Black Pearl. Though he promised to make a very grand beast, as big and powerful as his father, he had not the mysterious powers of Ben Josef and did not learn the strange language that Ali and Ben and Seyf the dwarf spoke together. That was a mystery that Ali understood in years to come – the strange secret of Ben Josef.

In truth Black Pearl, as far as his nature and wits were concerned, was just an ordinary camel, like other camels, excepting for the blackness of his coat and the cheerfulness of his heart. For the only gloomy thing about him was his colour, and he proved very good-tempered, willing, and friendly both with camels and men.

At last the wandering clan returned for a rest in the oasis, and his mother and father were very pleased to see the little house that Ali had built, largely with his own hands, for Morning Star. It had thick walls and a flat roof and was cool and pleasant. And Zaal had added some Arabic adornments to it, so that the dwelling proved a great addition to the oasis.

But next time Sheikh Heber travelled upon his territory and took his people with him into the sand, that they might live the roaming life they all loved, Ali and Morning Star went too, for they also were desert Arabs and could not stop in one place very long at a time.

Chapter XIII

◆

The Adventure of the Soul

Now a few years must slip by before we come to the end of this story, and they were years for Sheikh Heber and his people much like the years that everybody lives. You might think that after their splendid good fortune they were bound to get some bad luck, to balance things up, and so they did; but nothing serious or terrible happened to them and they jogged along pretty prosperously, while the time passed and the old folk dropped out and the young ones grew up to take their places. Sheikh Heber ruled with kindness and friendship for all his own people, and he was always ready and full of goodwill towards those whom he did not rule; and though Sheikh Khalid, being a fighting man, had occasional battles with other wandering tribes and sometimes won and sometimes lost them, he never dreamed of quarrelling with his dear friend at the oasis. The clans dwelt in closest kinship for evermore.

But, little by little, there rose a cloud upon the future, though it was a very long way off still, and Heber's wife said that it seemed a pity to meet trouble half-way. Heart's Delight was forty-six years old now and Heber was fifty years old, but strong and hearty still. And Ali was just thirty years old and a very fine man indeed, so there did not seem any particular reason to fear for the future chieftain of the tribe. But yet the trouble had to be faced. Heber must go presently, and then his son would become Sheikh Ali and reign over the clan; but who would follow Ali in years to come? Morning Star had no son to fill his father's shoes. She certainly bore three daughters, and nobody could have desired nicer daughters, for they were all lovely and all amazingly good. But Sheikh Heber began to worry about the far future and feel that Morning Star was making rather a tiresome habit of daughters, when it would be so much better if she tried something different and gave him a grandson for a change.

And after the third daughter was born, he began to take the matter rather seriously and feel that something must be done about it.

Now you will have seen in this story how brave the Arabs can be and what pluck they show and how they will fight and carry on against danger and bad fortune; but they are brave in all manner of ways and they are so tremendously and heroically brave that they will often marry two wives at once, or even more. Eastern people are as brave as that. King Solomon, for instance, was so terrifically brave that he married a hundred wives. They can only have had a very little bit of Solomon each; but at any rate he married a hundred girls; and no doubt they filled his palace pretty well, huge though it was. Some no doubt went in for dancing, and some for singing, and some for playing the sackbut; and some perhaps looked after the house, and some we must hope looked after Solomon; and all we may be sure wanted new, pretty clothes at least twice a week – to delight their brave, wise husband. But one thing they probably did not do, except the very cleverest of them, and that was to go off for holidays and give Solomon a rest now and then. Yet I am sure that if the whole hundred had all wanted to start for a change together, he would have been delighted to pack them off on a hundred camels – to the seaside, or the banks of the river Jordan, or the mountains of Lebanon, with their tents and pet dogs and games and toys for a long, long holiday. Because husbands – strange though it may sound – do love to have their palaces, or castles, or villas, or country houses, or town flats, or tents all to themselves sometimes; which is their funny notion of a holiday; and you may feel sure that Solomon would have dearly liked to be quite quiet and peaceful and utterly alone in Jerusalem now and then if he had got the chance.

But when Sheikh Heber told Ali that he must look round and get another wife and think about a son, Ali declared that he didn't want another wife at all, and spoke to Morning Star about it.

'You are, of course, quite brave enough to marry

another girl,' she said, 'and I am quite brave enough to let you marry a dozen; but you'd hate it really.'

'I'm sure I should,' replied Ali.

'The point is this,' continued Morning Star. 'You love me with every bit of love you have got – just as I love you – so if you married somebody else, there would be not a scrap of love left in your heart for her. And how dreadful that would be for the poor thing.'

'And for me,' declared Ali. 'In fact it would be worse than dreadful, because though it may seem very old-fashioned and behind the times, I have a strong feeling that you ought not to marry a girl unless you love her dearly and are prepared to go on loving her.'

'As to going on loving her,' replied Morning Star, 'you never can tell. When you married me, you couldn't be sure that you were going on loving me for ever, as you have done; but people certainly ought not to marry at all if they don't love one another in the least to start with.'

Yet Sheikh Heber went on feeling that something ought to be done about it, and finally Ali said that he would go and see Jameel.

'The Dreamer has been very good to our family,' he said, 'and given us many a helping hand in the past; so he may be able to do the like again.'

And Heber thought well of the idea, so presently Ali and Ben Josef set off for old Jameel once more. But they did not travel alone, because Ben wished that his son, Black Pearl, should go with them. Nobody knew why he wanted Black Pearl to go; but he knew very well and the reason appeared later on.

Black Pearl was now a magnificent camel, ten

years of age, and Ali was a splendid man; but of course Ben Josef had grown an old fellow and reached to the end of his life. He and Ali had celebrated their thirtieth birthday together and Ben knew that he was not going to have another birthday, for he was tired and ready to sleep his long sleep.

But, though the stages of his journeys had to be short and he needed plenty of rest between them, Ben Josef could still carry Ali safely, for his master, though strong as steel, was a light weight and put no strain upon him.

The three set off for the rose-red hills and Jameel's home, and Ali knew that the hermit would surely be expecting them. As they went the White Camel talked about his family and expressed a great regret that Black Pearl could not understand Ali, or take his place when he was gone.

'He will never be to you what I have been,' said Ben Josef, 'because something was left out of him and his mother.'

'No,' answered Ali, 'nothing was left out of him, or his mother that belongs to a good camel; but something was put into you that makes you different from all your kind. You are a Magic Camel, Ben, and always have been since you were born.'

'I suppose I must be,' answered Ben Josef. 'You are probably right, yet I can't understand it and never bother to try.'

'Perhaps Jameel could explain why you are magical,' answered Ali.

'It doesn't matter as long as I have satisfied you,' declared the White Camel. 'I have enjoyed a glorious life and wonderful good fortune; but things that had a beginning must always have an end whether they be good or bad, so enough said for the present.'

They took a long time getting to Jameel, for Ben Josef was very weary and didn't want anything to eat; but at last they arrived and were made welcome. The hermit began to grow tremendously old himself now, yet he was as active and tall and cheerful and chatty and pleasant as ever. They ate and drank, and Jameel admired Black Pearl greatly and said that he had never seen a nobler creature; and then, when Ben and his son had gone to sleep side by side under the stars, Ali talked to his ancient friend and put the two problems to him which were just now so difficult to answer. And Jameel listened very patiently.

'Two great things I am very anxious to know, dear Jameel,' began Ali, 'and one concerns me and the other concerns my beloved camel, Ben Josef. And I will put him first. Why is he unlike all other camels and what is that strange and magic thing in him which has made him my friend for thirty years and more, and enabled me to understand him and given him strength to understand me? That is the first interesting question, and the second is this. My father, Sheikh Heber, wants me to marry another wife, because Morning Star has no son; but I do not want another wife at all. A wife ought to be a pleasure; but if I married another wife, she would only be a duty, and it is dreadful to think of a wife as only a duty. Some duties are hard, but they are only hard on the man that struggles to do them and they turn into joy when he succeeds; but this would be a dreadful thing, not only for me but for a new wife, because it is perfectly certain that I shall never love her. I have my Morning Star, and there will never be any other star in the sky for me.'

Jameel did not reply at once when Ali had finished, but presently he spoke.

'These two problems,' he said, 'shall be answered together tomorrow, my son, for they are blended one with the other and can be solved together. I do not need to dream about them this time, because I already know all about them; and a very wonderful story they make. But something is going to happen tonight, and after it has happened I shall talk to you.'

'One more little question and I will trouble you no further,' said Ali. 'Why did Ben Josef bring Black Pearl with us? I asked him but he would not tell me. He said that I should know on the day after we came to you.'

'He was right,' replied Jameel. 'You will know tomorrow.'

Then they slept until the risen sun made the hills glow like a ring of fire round Jameel's home. And when Ali rose and went out to tend the camels, Black Pearl stood up on his mighty feet and shook himself and snorted the nightly dew out of his nostrils; but Ben Josef did not rise up, for he had passed away peacefully in his sleep and was no more.

Then Ali rent his coat and cried out and lamented, and Jameel came to him to calm him and tell him that all was well.

'I knew that he was going last night,' he said, 'and he knew that he was going. Here he shall lie and we will put his noble old body into the earth beside my house.'

So they dug deep to make a resting-place for the

White Camel, and as they dug together the hermit spoke in this manner.

'You may live close to the earth, like a violet, Ali, or you may tower high upon the air like an oleander, or a date palm; but you can be beautiful whether you live high or low. Nothing need be ugly. Indeed, a very great artist said that he had never seen an ugly thing in all his life; but that was because he owned a rare pair of eyes and a clear brain behind them. Your Ben Josef lived a beautiful life and died a beautiful death. You are poorer for the passing of Ben and will miss him yet treasure him in memory. He knew that his time was come and he knew that his journey to me would be his last journey. Therefore he brought Black Pearl to carry you home again. And when he has sunk into the sweet desert sand that he trod so grandly for thirty years, I will tell you his mystery and show you how strangely all has happened. Then you will praise Allah and cry "Kismet!" and be at peace.'

'Our coppersmith, Zaal, still makes beautiful things when he can spare the time,' replied Ali, 'and if I may bring him here, he shall cut a shaft of rosy granite from hill-top and set it above my Ben.'

'As to that,' replied Jameel, 'if you think again, Ali, you will think otherwise. Some creatures there always have been that desired their graves to be a pomp and show; and such there always will be. Abdullah, the great serpent, for example, would like a pyramid to stand above his ashes, that the world might know his greatness for ever. Not so Ben Josef. He would ask from us nothing better than the yellow sand, that he loved all his life, and a bunch of his favourite spurge growing upon it. And what more everlasting memorial than the spurge, for that has life and will endure as long as the Red Desert endures; but your pyramid is but a leaf in the hand of Time and, like a dead leaf, will fall.'

When all was done and their labour ended, Jameel spoke again and revealed for Ali the answer to both his questions; and then he understood.

'Some things that I shall tell you, Ali, you must believe, because, when you return to your people you will find that they have happened,' began the ancient man, 'but other things that I shall tell you cannot be proved, and you may believe or disbelieve them as you please.'

'I shall always believe you in future, whatever you say,' promised Ali.

'I am to speak of the Soul,' said Jameel, 'but no subject is more difficult and upon no subject do the minds of men differ so greatly. Now the Soul is a very important thing indeed in my opinion. People talk nonsense and say that they cannot call their souls their own, whereas the truth is quite otherwise, for you can always call your soul your own as long as you have it, no matter what happens to you. And it is your own in this way: it depends upon you only to make or mar it while it is with you. It is everlasting and therefore you cannot kill it; but you can treat it well, or ill, and much depends on that. For a soul may not stand still – it must go forward or backward; and if you are good to it, then it may go forward into something better presently, and if you treat it badly, it has to go backward into something not so good. Your soul has climbed upwards and upwards until it has reached you and belongs to you, who are a human being, and it is your business to help it higher still and make it worthy of a better house than yours. So, if you are all right, your soul will be all right; but if you are all wrong, then your soul will have to go down to a lower class in the school of life and start upward again.

'This, Ali, is what happened to the soul of your grandfather, Sheikh Abbas, because, though a very fine fellow and a grand fighter, he never looked after his soul properly. In a word he was not a good man and ruled by fear rather than love and never spoke the truth if a lie suited him better. So, when he died, his soul had to take a back seat for a time. It went down in the class and started life again in something not so grand as a man. At the moment Sheikh Abbas passed away, Ben Josef was born, and the old Sheikh's soul began another career in the White Camel. Do you see what happened?'

'Yes,' answered Ali. 'I quite see; and that is why, when he had to fight, old Ben fought so magnificently.'

'Exactly. That was a spark of Sheikh Abbas coming out in Ben. But the grand thing is this. Ben Josef was such a rare, good, faithful camel that after thirty years with him, his soul is in fine form again and ready to go forward and upward once more. And his soul has gone forward, and when it left him took a step upward once again.'

'Where has it gone now?' asked Ali.

'Into fruitful soil we will hope,' replied Jameel, 'and when you return home all your questions will be answered and you will understand the whole story.'

So Ali, knowing now to trust the Dreamer's queer speeches, put faith in what he had been told, thanked

Jameel, set a fine plant of spurge upon Ben Josef's grave and, then started off homeward upon Black Pearl.

As he had done long ago, Seyf came out to meet him from the oasis with news. Seyf was getting a pretty elderly dwarf now, but he still enjoyed life, though he spent most of it in idleness.

When he saw Ali on the black camel he cried out to know where Ben Josef might be, and wept when he heard that he had passed away.

'He was a great friend, and I shall miss him very much,' said Seyf. 'All the magic seems to be going out of the world nowadays, and what is a world without a pinch of magic?'

And then he told Ali that Morning Star had brought a son into the world; and so Ali guessed what had happened.

When he sat with his mother and father that night he tried to explain the mystery to them and let them understand that Ben Josef's soul had taken a step upward again and was now, without doubt, looking at them through the brown eyes of Morning Star's baby; but Sheikh Heber felt very foggy about it.

'I am a simple, plain man,' he said, 'and do not understand these mysteries. They are beyond my wits, and I should fear that ancient Jameel has made it all up and was talking nonsense.'

But Heart's Delight, Ali's mother, believed every word of the story.

'I think it is a splendid piece of news,' she said to him, 'for you and your father are such a gentle, peace-loving pair, that to get the soul of fierce old Sheikh Abbas back again into the family is a most excellent thing. We never know what stern future may lie in store for us.'

'Now that I consider it, the child certainly reveals a very firm mouth and the eyes of a young hawk,' admitted Sheikh Heber, 'and Morning Star says that he has the making of a tyrant already.'

'You are both dear good fellows,' answered his wife, 'and love the answer that turns away wrath. If you could make the world nearer to your heart's desire, I am sure it would be a much nicer place than it is. But you cannot do that, or bring back those old days, when the Arabs were less busy and discontented and unhappy than they seem to be now.'

'All great nations have had cause to sigh for the passing of their Golden Ages,' said Heber, 'and we Arabs among the rest. But let us not sigh for the precious past; let us rather laugh at the thought of a still more precious future – a future bright and brighter as it comes to gladden the hills of dawn. And let each of us do our little best to hasten a new and grander Golden Age that all people of the earth shall share.'

'You are really almost too good for this world, darling,' answered Heart's Delight; 'but we must be practical as well as good; and I still hope that Morning Star's baby will have a streak of something pretty tough in him. For the deeds that will cry to be done in the future must surely need a knife with a cutting blade as well as a golden handle.'

'What are you going to call your boy, Ali?' asked his father.

'I am going to call him after his great-grandfather: Abbas.'

'So history goes round in a circle, like a kitten playing with its tail,' said Sheikh Heber.

And then they all went to bed.

YOUNG SPITFIRE'S

Bows Against the Barons

by Geoffrey Trease

The tale of young Dickon – made an outlaw for killing one of the king's deer – and his fight against injustice. This classic work captures the clash between rich and poor, and above all, the story of the great leader, Robin Hood of Sherwood Forest – presented as the author felt he really might have been.

ISBN 1 904027 26 1   156pp   Paperback   £6.99

The Viper of Milan

by Marjorie Bowen

Set in fourteenth-century Italy, the story is about the enmity between two princes, Visconti, the evil Duke of Milan and Mastino della Scala, the dispossessed Duke of Verona. The hatred of these two men is the absorbing basis of the plot, but the vivid descriptions of Milan and the countryside, and the almost unbelievable cruelty and black-heartedness of the unscrupulous Visconti, help to make the impact of this story a really tremendous one.

ISBN 1 904027 24 5   274pp   Paperback   £9.99

John Diamond

by Leon Garfield

Narrated with verve and pace by a master story-teller, John Diamond follows the quest of William Jones and his heart-stopping adventures through the streets of a richly-imagined eighteenth-century London. With a cast of characters worthy of Charles Dickens, John Diamond was the winner of the Whitbread Award and the Boston Globe–Horn Book Award.

ISBN 1 904027 32 6   208pp   Paperback   £7.99

Published in Great Britain by

Elliott & Thompson Ltd
27 John Street
London WC1N 2BX

First published 1936

Text & Illustrations
© The Royal Literary Fund 2004

ISBN 1 904027 25 3

First edition

Book design by Brad Thompson
Printed and bound in Malta by Interprint